PRAISE FOR *HOOKED*

"This is the perfect blend of science and experience rolled into an educational and practical exploration of addiction. I couldn't put it down."
Shona Vertue, bestselling author of *The Vertue Method*

"Shame lives in the dark and dies in the light. Finally, a spectacular book bringing it to the light."
Morgane Polanski, actor and director

"There is something in this book for everyone to learn, even if you didn't know you needed it."
Holly Ramsay, mental health advocate

TALITHA FOSH

FOREWORD BY ADWOA ABOAH

HOOKED

WHY WE ARE ADDICTED AND HOW TO BREAK FREE

AMARYLLIS

AMARYLLIS

An imprint of Manjul Publishing House Pvt. Ltd.
• C-16, Sector 3, Noida, Uttar Pradesh 201301, India
Website: www.manjulindia.com
Registered Office:
• 2nd Floor, Usha Preet Complex, 42 Malviya Nagar, Bhopal 462 003 – India
Distribution Centres
Ahmedabad, Bengaluru, Chennai, Hyderabad,
Kochi, Kolkata, Mumbai, Noida, Pune

Hooked by Talitha Fosh

First published in the UK and USA in 2024 by Watkins,
an imprint of Watkins Media Limited
watkinspublishing.com

First published in paperback in India in 2025

ISBN 978-93-5543-483-8

Printed and bound in India by Repro India Limited

CONTENTS

FOREWORD

BY ADWOA ABOAH

When I met Tally in an addiction treatment centre in 2014, we formed an instant friendship at a time in my life when I needed it most. It was a connection and a bond that was rooted in authenticity, integrity, honesty and respect. These were all things that were lacking in my life at the time.

Meeting her was a pivotal moment; our relationship taught me what true friendship and connection should look like. It took years of trial and error to bring this into my other relationships, but Tally's friendship was definitely the starting block of everything I know to be true now. It's my foundation, the thing I return to time and time again. It's the proof I needed that, if we're open to it, through honesty, understanding, empathy and respect, we can meet our people, our community, even in times of great sadness and darkness. Ones who will not judge us but meet us where we're at, celebrate us, love us and support us.

At first glance, Tally and I didn't have much in common. As humans, we judge others too quickly for things that don't really matter. We were both from different backgrounds, and we had different interests – factors we often used to stop ourselves looking outside our social box. However, when you are thrust into these weird situations – places like rehab – you do not have the space to be judgemental or picky about who you hang out with.

I think we are all looking to feel less alone – in our circumstances, in our problems and in our shit. Because, when you are in the thick of it, you think you are the only person on the planet going through those particular things. And then you hear someone's story – like Tally's story in this book – and you soon realize that couldn't be further from the truth.

It's validating when you see yourself reflected in someone else's tale, someone who lives a life completely different from your own. When they speak their truth from a place of vulnerability and authenticity, and it resonates with you, and you see yourself in it – it makes you feel less alone. And that's what Tally does in these pages: she makes me feel less alone.

Addiction doesn't pick you because of your economic status or background. Anyone can be subjected to its horrors. But because of the world that we live in, access to help and resources are only offered to those more fortunate. Even the word addiction is still so stigmatized, viewed in such a black-and-white way. As humans, we lack empathy and understanding, we're quick to judge and we never listen. However, it is open dialogue, language, storytelling and books like this that can change the way we look at addiction and how we treat those in the grips of active addiction.

You should listen to Tally's story if you need community, if you are in need of truth and you want to hear from someone who is going to speak from a place of authenticity. Someone who is not going to embellish it, and from someone who has had to do such a huge amount of work on themselves to get to who they are now.

Tally, I am so grateful for you. May your story inspire others to create their own community that supports them on the journey they're about to take.

INTRODUCTION

So many of us are addicts. In modern society, it is almost impossible not to be one. Television, cinema, social media, apps and games are all jostling for our attention. They want us to spend every second of our waking hours interacting with their content: liking, subscribing, binging, browsing, gaming or gambling.

Today we have emails to reply to, letters, voicemails, texts and DMs (Direct Messaging). Traditional advertising and social media influencers tell us how to look, what to wear and how to feel. When we come home from a long day at work or school, or after a day of looking after a toddler, anything that can take our minds off our worries for a couple of hours looks enticing. Scrolling through a social media feed, having a drink, smoking a cigarette or binging on sugar can all help us cope. But this can come at a cost.

Our brains haven't caught up with the 21st century. They weren't ready for this onslaught of stimulation. Pathways in the brain that we have developed over millions of years to encourage us to eat, sleep and have sex have now been hijacked by drugs, smartphones and calorie-rich food. As a result, our brains develop a hunger for these stimuli and command us to seek them again and again.

I define addiction as using something outside of yourself to change the way you feel. Therefore, I challenge the image of the stereotypical addict: the person who is constantly stumbling around drunk, shooting up in a derelict house or stealing to pay off their gambling debts. Yes, there are people who unfortunately find themselves in these situations, but I view addiction as a sliding scale. We often use substances or behaviours to cope with our anxiety, our anger or our fears. I would argue that if we continue to use these, despite them negatively impacting our lives, we are addicted. The severity of our addiction and the negative consequences can vary from person to person.

Do you find yourself staying up past your bedtime scrolling through TikTok because you want to have just a few hours numb to your stress? Have you missed social occasions because you want to complete a video game and feel some achievement? Do you drink to relieve social anxiety but always find yourself getting out of control? These are situations you might want to reflect on, and this book offers guidance on how to do just that.

Since the beginning of the COVID-19 pandemic, we experienced a change in the world whereby we were forced to sit still with ourselves. For a lot of us, this was extremely challenging, as it was perhaps the first time we were ever really still, without all the distractions of our usual busy lives.

When was the last time you sat quietly or went for a walk without any background noise? Sitting with just ourselves is something that might feel quite alien to some people. It means we must pay attention to our thoughts or our feelings, and that can be confronting. Instead, we listen to the radio, put on a podcast or have a drink.

Pre-COVID, we had the ability to distract ourselves, consciously or not, by leading busy lives – seeing friends, going out, spending time at the office, drinking or partying. We had little time for introspection. People were shocked by how difficult it is to be still and look inward. For the first time, many people found they had to ask themselves questions they had been avoiding for a very long time. I believe this caused addictive behaviours, such as drinking, drug-taking and eating disorders, to increase when COVID-19 started.

Constantly distracting ourselves from our thoughts means that we cannot identify or pay attention to a potential wound within us: our worries, our negative beliefs about ourselves, the shame we hold and the carried shame passed down by our family. However, our addictive behaviours are merely a bandage.

Identifying this is the first step in making lasting, beneficial change. Instead of putting a bandage over how we feel, breaking our habits allows us to let the wound itself heal. Replacing these quick, addictive solutions with long-lasting, fulfilling activities can lead to both physical and mental health improvements and a sense of contentment I once never thought was possible.

This book will explore the origins of addiction, map its natural course and dismantle the stereotype of the "addict". It will outline the highs these addictive behaviours bring, dissect why these highs will never be enough, and uncover the lows. It will describe the barriers to change, explain why we often are in denial about our use, and shed light on the negative, sometimes devastating, consequences of our addictions. Through case studies, exercises and reflections, you will be able to recognize any potentially addictive behaviours you practice, identify their perceived benefits and come to terms with what they are distracting you from. These exercises will explore your deeper feelings and help you sit with yourself. They will provide you with the tools to take better care of yourself, break your unhealthy habits and lay the foundation for any therapy you may choose to pursue. You will be encouraged to write down or even draw your thoughts and feelings, and reflect on the topics we explore. With that in mind, I recommend keeping a blank, dedicated journal close by.

But you don't need to go it alone. We will cover what assistance is available, whether it be speaking to family and friends, peer support groups or therapists. Most importantly, we will talk about how to ask for help.

Many addiction therapists are addicts in recovery. I am no exception. In the appendix to this book, you'll find a letter my mother wrote to me when I was in rehab. Here she describes my addiction as a monster. A monster that was breathtakingly self-obsessed. This monster made me steal from her, lived for drama and selfies, and was constantly hungry for likes.

I started drinking alcohol at the age of 15. It gave me the confidence that I had been searching for my whole life. As I got older, I began drinking at every social occasion. I would take things too far, kiss people I shouldn't have kissed and say things I shouldn't have said. I would feel hungover, anxious and guilty the next day. I would then drink again to make me feel better about myself, and the cycle would repeat. My mother's friend took me to an Alcoholics Anonymous (AA) meeting when I was 17, and I couldn't wait to get out of there. At 20, I started using cocaine, which really escalated things. This addictive cycle became an addictive spiral. The worsening self-loathing and the misery I felt led me to want to end my life.

Thankfully for me, I had great support from those around me, and I was lucky to receive treatment. I had fully surrendered and agreed to attend regular AA meetings and an outpatient treatment centre.

Unfortunately, soon after I stopped drinking, my dormant eating disorder reared its head. I was diagnosed with anorexia at 14 after I began restricting my food. I would also binge and purge. I returned to the same treatment centre only six months after being discharged. That still wasn't enough. Due to my rapid weight loss, I was sent to an eating disorder treatment centre in South Africa for five months.

However, through engaging in therapy, practicing mindfulness, creating new habits, surrounding myself with a support circle and completing my yoga teacher training, I am happy to say that I am now nine years sober, and my eating has been extremely stable. I use the word stable because recovery is not straightforward. It is a journey and a process that is never perfect.

When I got back from South Africa, I realized I might be able to help people with struggles similar to mine. I started with a foundation course in counselling and, following this, ended up doing another three years of training in counselling and psychotherapy. At the end of my training, I went back to work at the rehabilitation centre that I had been in myself. I have also been an AA sponsor and have developed my own practice.

I work with a wide range of clients, including those experiencing bereavement, anxiety and depression, and I run seminars on love addiction and attachment styles. However, a significant proportion of my clients are suffering with addictions or eating disorders.

I understand first-hand the nature of the addictive cycle, the shame we can feel to admit there is a problem, and how easy it is to minimize our own suffering. I know the feeling of being stuck and unable to see a way out, and I'm familiar with self-loathing. I know how painful and destructive addiction can be. But I also know that recovery is possible, that a new outlook and a new way of living is achievable.

At one time I genuinely believed that my life was destined to fulfil these self-destructive patterns. I never thought I would get to a place of valuing and looking after myself. It was only when I heard stories from people who had given up alcohol or let go of their eating disorder that I began to hope. They had gained freedom from the incessant nature of a negative or critical mind, and it made me believe that I could achieve this freedom and find peace as well. I hope that this book is that story for you. Although I was lucky to receive the treatment I did, I am not special or different – I know you can do it too.

Throughout my journey, I have spoken to my peers at treatment centres and AA meetings, to friends who have been struggling, to contemporaries who have relapsed and to countless therapists. I have participated in one-on-one counselling, group therapy, art therapy and music therapy. As a therapist, I have learned from my colleagues, I have researched and absorbed from great minds referenced in this book and I have experience in guiding people to recovery.

The contents of this book are based on what I've learned from being both client and therapist. Although I was toward the extreme end of the addiction spectrum, these theories and exercises can be applied by anyone who wants to make a positive change, however small. I am as susceptible to scrolling through social media as everyone else, but I now have an awareness that I'm doing it, I can understand the reasons why I'm doing it and I can address it before it impacts my day.

The one thing I want you to promise yourself when you start this journey is to be kind to yourself. This will help you get the best out of the following exercises. There is no need to judge or beat yourself up. You are taking the first steps into new territory!

If so many of us are addicts, first we'd better look at what addiction really is and how we become addicts in the first place. Let's dive in.

CHAPTER 1
WHAT IS ADDICTION?

What Does it Mean to Be an Addict?

I had a client, N, who spent a lot of time on dating apps. He had been on a fair number of dates, but they had never progressed into a relationship.

"I don't think I even want to go on the date," he explained.

So why does he go on the apps?

"It helps my self-esteem. If I get a match, then I don't feel bad about myself – it means I could go on a date if I wanted."

We then explored if there were any negative consequences of spending time on dating apps. How much time was it?

"I don't know, maybe an hour? Sometimes I tell myself ten more swipes, but then I get to ten, and then I go for another ten, and so on ... "

So what were the negative consequences?

"My thumb hurts from swiping. But if I am really honest, I think it has probably ruined my love life. When I go on a date with someone, I just think I could probably match with someone new who might be better."

After reading the above conversation, would you say that N is addicted to dating apps? He can't put them down, he has some physical pain and it seems to have a negative impact on forming new relationships. But if you'd only just met N, I'm not sure you'd suspect N of having an addiction. He works in finance, exercises three times a week, has a good group of friends and comes across as an affable person.

You might have an idea of what an addict looks like or should look like. But I want to emphasize that anyone can have an addiction, and they are a lot more common than you think.

In this chapter, I will talk about addiction in a general sense. What it means to be addicted and how we can dismantle the taboo of addiction. Why is it important to do so? Like with many mental health conditions, addiction comes with a certain stigma or stereotype. However, like with my client N, addictive behaviours can affect people with a seemingly "normal" life. The negative connotations associated with addiction often mean we either hide or are ashamed of it. But that doesn't need to be the case! If we think we might be addicted to something, that is a good first step. It means we have identified an aspect of our behaviour that we can improve and work on. I hope this book can open up conversations on the topic and create a safer space for everyone who might be struggling. When reading this chapter, I encourage you to come at it with an open mind, without judgement for yourself or anyone else.

The Taboo of Addiction

Before we go any further, I want you to find a blank piece of paper in your journal. Write out any words that you associate with the term *addiction*. They can be words you have heard others say or just what you believe addiction to be. Try not to filter your writing; you don't need to share these thoughts with anyone. It's merely to see if you have any prejudices around addiction that we can challenge. I want to ask why you think these things about addiction. Where do they come from?

When I asked a few people what they associate with the word addiction, their words were: "helpless", "dependence", "destruction", "loss of control", "obsession", "hurt", "craving", "compulsion" and "fixation".

In our society, the word addiction has had very negative connotations. From Mark Twain's Papp Finn – the abusive, drunken father – to *The Simpsons*' Barney Gumble, society has forever depicted people with addiction as those who are living on the street or can't get out of bed without first having a drink. People who create havoc in their own lives. Like *EastEnders*' Lisa Fowler, we envision gambling addicts as those who blackmail others for money to fund their addiction. Or we imagine that all those with eating disorders are only skin and bone. While all these things can certainly happen in active addiction, these are extreme cases, and we are mostly unaware that our addictive behaviours can be much more subtle and insidious.

Like with Barney Gumble, sometimes these depictions can lack compassion and an understanding of why the person is addicted. We assume that the person's addiction struggle is about their lack of willpower. We assume that the label "addiction" means there is something inherently wrong with a person, and we don't necessarily understand that addiction is an illness that we can recover from.

Growing up, I certainly had these negative associations with addiction. I had only been taught to fear the word or not to associate with it. I remember at school having talks on drugs, only to be told how bad they were and how bad I would be if I decided to engage with them ... because, God forbid, I might become an addict.

Addiction is not something people choose to have; it can be something we live with for ever. Some people in the addiction space suggest that we shouldn't be encouraging the phrase "I am an addict", as it reinforces the addiction. If someone describes themselves as an addict all the time, it means they will stay stuck or use the fact they have an addiction as an excuse for their behaviour.

While I agree that it is very important to look at how we talk to ourselves and the labels we use to describe ourselves, I feel that being an addict shouldn't cause feelings of shame. I think by not identifying ourselves with the word "addict", we are only exacerbating the problem that society already has by trying to keep it hush hush. Getting to this place has taken me a while, but I find it quite liberating to acknowledge that I am an addict. I don't think it defines me; it is something I have suffered with, but I am grateful for what it has taught me and the U-turn my life took as a result of my addiction.

Addiction is also not something that we can "get rid of", and therefore, it is much healthier to accept we are an addict and understand that we can live in recovery from it, as opposed to simply getting rid of it. When working with clients who struggle with addiction, one of the first things I do is get them to find a name for their addiction. Any name they feel is appropriate! One client labels their addiction "Jack" (after Jack Daniels), and another labels their addiction "the beast". This helps them understand that they are not their addiction. Some clients see it as a devil-like figure that lives on their shoulder, always tempting them toward self-destructive behaviours. Usually, when the client is able to understand that they are not their addiction, they feel a separation from it and slowly come to terms with the fact that it isn't their fault and they are not inherently bad people. This can help with the feelings of shame and self-loathing intertwined with all the addictive behaviours.

This exercise can also work if you suffer with intrusive thoughts or a strong critical inner voice. I want you to think of a name for the voice that lives inside your head and tells you that you're not good enough. Or the voice that makes you feel like you're an imposter at work or with your friends. Mine is called Lexi. And when I am feeling tired or vulnerable, Lexi definitely still makes herself known. But having her as a separate person in my head helps me politely tell her to leave me alone, or sometimes, to just shut up! Although it took a number of years to get her completely under control, in the early stages, the more I practised challenging her, the easier it became.

For me personally, it's important that I acknowledge I am an addict and always will be an addict. Now, I don't use this as a reason to beat myself up or to lean on as an excuse for my sometimes-self-destructive behaviour, but the times my head tells me that I can just have one drink, I have to remind myself that I am an addict and can't just have one drink. It would have dangerous consequences for me. Paul Merson, an ex-football player who struggled with his gambling addiction for many years, talks about the idea of addiction being simply due to a lack of willpower. He compared addiction to having a disease like a stomach bug. What really made me laugh was when he said once on a podcast, "Stop diarrhoea with willpower, and let me know how you get on."[1] It's the same thing with addiction – it's an illness, and it takes more than willpower to stop engaging in addictive behaviours.

What Makes Me an Addict?

What does the word *addiction* actually mean? The definition according to the *Oxford English Dictionary* is "The state of dependence produced either by the habitual taking of drugs, or by regularly engaging in certain behaviours, e.g., gambling."[2] While this might be the literal meaning of the word, to me, the way I define addiction is "When we seek something external to change the way we feel internally."

In 1956, the American Medical Association classified alcoholism as a disease, and in 1987 they also included addiction as a disease. Then, in 2011, the American Society of Addiction Medicine joined the American Medical Association in defining addiction as a chronic brain disorder.[3] Addiction was no longer recognized as just a behavioural problem or the result of making bad choices.

Although there is a stigma of drug use being abnormal or "bad", we often use drugs in our day-to-day lives. We can have a drink with friends in the pub or take medication that our doctor prescribes to us. Therefore, the use of drugs does not mean someone is a junkie. Humans have used substances for millennia for a multitude of reasons. From the use of the mushroom Amanita in Central Asia for religious ceremonies and the passing of a ceremonial pipe of the Indigenous peoples of the Americas to the use of opium for medicinal purposes, our relationship with drugs goes beyond purely substance and user. How we view them is influenced by our culture, society, religious beliefs, individual psychology and genetics.[4]

So, when do we say we are addicted to something? What if addiction doesn't show up for us in an obvious and painful way? For me, put very simply, addiction is when a substance or behaviour starts to make our lives unmanageable.

What does an unmanageable life look like? Well, when our behaviours negatively affect our day-to-day lives. For example, missing work, letting friends down, not being able to take care of ourselves (including not getting enough sleep). Unmanageability means that we break promises or boundaries, even those we make with ourselves. Even when we realize something is a problem, we keep doing it.

For me, my addiction caused me to miss work or not wake up on time in the morning. Also, who I became when I was drinking was not someone I was proud of. The way drinking made me feel about myself brought me to my knees. The self-loathing I felt meant that I didn't feel able to go out socially without getting drunk. This was all part of the shame cycle I found myself in.

Calling in sick to work and missing flights because I had slept through my alarm after a late night went on for years. Eventually, when it all came to a head about ten years ago, I felt so worthless that I didn't want to carry on living. I will never forget this period of three days I had in bed after a big weekend where I was contemplating ending my own life. Nothing in particular had happened that was any different to my average weekend, but I had just had enough. I was fed up of being sick and tired. I felt that if I didn't do something about the way my life was, I wouldn't want to continue with it.

This eventually brought me to a therapist who knew exactly what I was struggling with and knew that I needed a gentle push toward removing alcohol from my life. I said that I was desperate and willing to do whatever it took to not feel like this anymore. He recommended an outpatient treatment programme at a rehab centre in London called Start2Stop. He said that throughout the duration of this programme, I wouldn't be allowed to drink, and because I was so desperate, I agreed. In Alcoholics Anonymous (AA) they call it the "gift of desperation" when you feel you are at such a rock bottom that you are willing to change. This really was my experience. My desperation was a gift that got me to finally let go and do something differently.

IDENTIFYING UNMANAGEABILITY

Grab your journal or a piece of paper. I want you to write down any times you have found your life becoming unmanageable because of a certain behaviour. Have a think about whether you've ever set yourself a boundary or made yourself a promise that you couldn't stick to. Note down any occasions that come to mind.

This exercise doesn't have to be related to drugs or alcohol. I've added some other examples below and some questions to think about for each one.

- **Social Media:** Do you find yourself scrolling endlessly and feeling like you can't stop even though your eyes feel tired and heavy? Have you ever sabotaged your sleep to stay up and watch more TikTok videos?
- **Shopping:** Do you sometimes have lots to do but find yourself procrastinating by shopping online, and hours go by and you don't understand where the time has gone?

- **Gaming:** Have you ever planned something with friends but then bailed because you'd rather be at home gaming?
- **Food:** Have you ever been dishonest with your friends and family about your eating habits, for example telling them you've already eaten because you don't want to have dinner for fear of gaining weight?

This exercise can help us identify any behaviours we previously considered normal or believed to be inconsequential. Anything you have identified may be something to reflect on as we progress through the book.

We are going to talk about the different types of addiction soon. But first I want to look a bit more closely at alcoholism as an example. It is certainly a more widely understood addiction in society and in research. Being an alcoholic myself, I also have first-hand experience. One misconception about alcoholism is that someone can only be an alcoholic if they drink bottles and bottles a day. However, this isn't necessarily what makes one an addict. The problem for the addict often occurs when they have had their first sip of alcohol. If an addict just has one sip, they cannot safely say when they will stop.

The issue lies in the fact that sometimes addicts can have just one drink. One night, we will go to the bar to have just one, and successfully have just one. However, oftentimes we say we will have just one and end up in blackout – that is the danger.

The addiction to alcohol is also known as an "allergy" to alcohol. You might drink the same amount as everyone else, but it seems to have a different effect on you than on other people. For example, you could completely change in personality when you have had a few drinks.

The same can be said for other addictions too – the way that the brain of an addict is wired means that engaging in addictive behaviour has a different effect on their brain chemistry compared to non-addicts. Their addictive behaviour patterns can then make their life unmanageable.

In our culture, there is a big emphasis on binge drinking. We tell ourselves that during the week we shouldn't drink, but on weekends we can let loose. We assume that because we aren't drinking every day, we can't possibly be alcoholics.

However, there lies an addictive cycle within this binge pattern – when it comes to the weekend, we are totally out of control. There is an aspect of having our "reward" as we have been so good during the week. Examples of unmanageability could be spending the whole of our weekend in bed hungover or being unable to show up at important family functions.

Addictive Behaviour Checklist

I have created a checklist with the below questions that will help you gain insight if you find yourself repeating the same addictive patterns. Go easy on yourself – all you have to do is be honest to the best of your ability, bearing in mind these questions might feel confronting.

The following questions are adapted from Alcoholics Anonymous, and they just require a yes or no answer:

1 Have you ever decided to stop your addictive habit (drinking, gambling, binging, shopping, smoking, social media, exercise, gaming, etc.) for a week but only lasted a few days?
2 Do you wish people would mind their own business about your addictive behaviour and stop telling you what to do?
3 Have your addictive behaviours resulted in your inability to meet your obligations at work, home or school?
4 Have you cut back or abandoned social, recreational or professional activities due to your addictive behaviour?

5 Have you experienced social or relationship problems due to your addictive behaviour?
6 Have you kept engaging with your addictive behaviour even though you experience worsening physical or mental health?
7 Have you ever felt like your life would be better if you didn't engage in your addictive behaviour?
8 Do you ever tell yourself you can stop your addictive behaviour whenever you want to but find yourself engaging in the behaviour even when you don't mean to?
9 Has your addictive behaviour caused you trouble at home?
10 Do you envy people who can drink/eat/game/gamble/ enjoy relationships without getting into trouble?
11 Do you ever engage in your addictive behaviour as soon as you wake up?
12 Do you ever feel ashamed or guilty after engaging in your addictive behaviour?

Have you answered yes to some of these questions?[5] If so, it is possible that you are engaging in a destructive addictive behaviour. Please don't panic – it is good to be aware of this, and it might be the platform for you to make lasting change.

Also, you are not alone! I created a survey with similar questions that I sent out to around 50 people who don't necessarily identify as addicts. A full 100 per cent of the participants said that they had at some point used something outside of themselves to change the way they feel, and when they then tried to take a break from a harmful behaviour or substance, they returned to it quicker than they initially set out. I would hesitate to label all these people addicts, but the key is the unmanageability of their behaviour and whether it negatively impacts their lives.

If you don't identify with any of the above questions, that's totally okay. Perhaps you are looking at them through the lens of a loved one's addictive behaviours. If that's the case, then you can simply ask these questions about them to see if there are any addictive patterns in their behaviour. Either way, this book will give you the tools to help you and your loved one tackle these behaviours, and I'll also suggest ways you can look after yourselves in the process.

How Do We Become Addicted?

Why do some people become addicts while some do not? Unfortunately, there isn't really a simple answer.

For many years there has been an argument about what causes someone to become addicted. You may have heard of nature versus nurture. Nature refers to our DNA, the genes passed down from our parents – for example, hair colour or eye colour. Nurture refers to things that are coded into us through early childhood interactions and the environment around us – what we feel about ourselves, about the world and about other people.

It is estimated that nature and nurture have a roughly equal impact on your risk of developing addictions to alcohol, nicotine or other drugs.[6]

Nature

There is no one gene to blame for someone becoming addicted. However, some genes have been identified as increasing the likelihood that someone will become addicted to something. Sometimes several genes can work together to influence the probability of someone becoming an addict.

For example, over 100 scientists collected information from a database of 1.2 million people to look at their smoking (when did they start, how much did they smoke, when did they stop, etc.) and alcohol use (drinks per week, etc.). They then compared this data to specific genes that were suspected to be involved in substance abuse. From this comparison, they were able to locate over 400 locations in the human genome that might influence smoking and alcohol use. Some of these genes in the genome code for how nerves send signals to each other and how dopamine is released in our brains (this can give us a high). This might help us understand how these genes make addiction more likely. Three genes in particular stood out: CUL3, PDE4B and PTGER3.[7]

Another study showed that some people have a genetic disposition to find a certain chemical – 6-n-Propylthiouracil (PROP) – more bitter than others do. If people find PROP bitter, they often find ethanol, some beers and red wine bitter too. Not only this, but they seem to have more taste buds. Those who don't find PROP bitter may also not experience the burning sensation from drinking a shot. In the study, people who found PROP less bitter were the people who tended to drink more alcohol.[8]

Some other specific genes have been identified that may increase/decrease the likelihood of addiction:

- **GABRA2 and CHRM2:** Associations between these genes and alcohol dependence have been identified in multiple studies. These genes are also associated with earlier-onset alcohol abuse as well as having other drug-related addictions.[9]
- **DRD2:** The A1 form (allele) of the dopamine receptor gene DRD2 in our brains is more common in people addicted to alcohol, cannabis, heroin, cocaine and nicotine. It is thought to be linked to a defect in the brain's reward mechanisms. It is also associated with impulse and compulsive behaviours such as attention deficit/hyperactivity disorder (ADHD), Tourette's syndrome, autism, pathological gambling and sex addiction. This gene is linked to a theory called the reward deficiency syndrome, where the brain is more resistant to dopamine (the "feel good" chemical). The lack of response these people have to the normal doses of dopamine mean they receive less enjoyment from ordinary

life. As a result they may look to other external sources of pleasure such as addictive substances.[10 11 12]

- **ALDH2*2:** This gene causes an enzyme in the body to not break down alcohol properly and results in a build-up of toxic chemicals. This makes people with this gene experience nausea, facial flushing, headaches and a rapid heartbeat when they drink alcohol. The gene therefore protects them from developing alcoholism. [13 14]

Nurture

When it comes to nurture, there are also many factors that contribute to someone becoming an addict. It's common to beat ourselves up as we think we have control over our nurture, but in actual fact, we have as much control over it as over our genetics – zero.

As we go through life, there are many different things that can impact our filter (the way that we see the world). This stems a lot from our belief systems that are created when we are young, and we carry them with us throughout our lives. If we have negative belief systems because we weren't nurtured the way we needed, we will carry this into our adult lives. This could manifest in anxiety, low self-confidence or a desire to look externally toward addictive behaviours to soothe how we feel internally.

In America, the Adverse Childhood Experiences study gathered data from over 17,000 people regarding historical difficulties they had in childhood. These adverse childhood experiences (ACE) included:

- **Abuse:** Emotional, physical and sexual
- **Household Challenges:** Domestic violence, substance abuse or mental illness in the household, parental separation or divorce, incarcerated household member
- **Neglect:** Emotional and physical

They found that two thirds of the participants experienced at least one ACE and more than one in six had four or more ACEs.

Following this, the number of adverse childhood experiences were compared to the mental and physical health of the person surveyed. Findings showed that people who had four or more ACEs were twice as likely to smoke, seven times more likely to be addicted to alcohol, ten times more likely to inject drugs and twelve times more likely to have had a suicide attempt.[15 16]

When I read this study, I was shocked at how common these ACEs were, but sadly it does reflect the experiences of my clients. One common theme I hear from them, despite the differing experiences and the differing struggles and addictions, is shame.

Shame and Addiction

My definition of shame is a feeling of being wrong, a deep feeling of self-loathing and worthlessness. No matter what we achieve in our lives, if we suffer with shame, nothing will ever be good enough, and we will find it very hard to celebrate ourselves. The way I like to describe shame is in comparison to guilt. Guilt is a feeling of "I have done wrong", whereas shame is a feeling of "I am wrong".

For me, shame manifested as a physical sensation of being dirty. Feeling disgusted with myself sometimes felt so physical that I had the sensation of wanting to scratch my skin off.

But what has this got to do with addiction? Shame is one of the strongest emotions that underlies any addiction. Why? Well, to put it simply, if we feel shame, we develop negative belief systems and are much more likely to behave in ways that are self-destructive. If we feel a sense of being wrong deep down, we are going to automatically – perhaps even unconsciously – make harmful choices for ourselves. Why would we be kind to ourselves if we feel worthless, right?

Destructive shame perpetuates whatever addictive cycle we find ourselves in. As long as we feel shame, we will continue to seek addictive behaviours.

Where Does Shame Come From?

Shame can be hard to identify as a nurture element in the development of an addiction. It is rather insidious because we carry it with us from way back when we were tiny. We do not come out of the womb with shame, but it is something that starts at an early age, develops and embeds itself in us as we grow up.

British psychologist and psychiatrist John Bowlby, who is widely known for his pioneering work in attachment theory, regularly talked about a baby developing an internal model of itself and others based on its early interactions. That feeling of not being quite good enough and being unlovable comes from not having its needs met. The resulting shame sits there within you and means you can't really show your true self.

As babies, we are constantly being programmed during these early interactions with our parents. If a baby has an available mother who soothes them, that baby will internalize that ability to soothe and, over time, learn how to self-soothe. If the mother is not readily available, then the baby will not learn this and will instead have feelings of shame and a lack of self-worth.

Then, between the ages of 8 and 12, we develop a sense of self – who we are, what we like, what we don't like, how we interact with our peers, etc. It is also very important during this period that both our emotional and physical needs are met. If, for whatever reason, our needs aren't met during this period, we may internalize it in a way that there is something wrong with us. This contributes to our feelings of shame.

Here's an example of an emotional need not being met. Let's say we are eight years old and someone at school told us they didn't like our sneakers. We may be upset because we really like them – they're new and we went to pick them out at the weekend. We come home and express our feelings to our caregivers or parents, but we are told not to be silly or not to cry. This minimizes our reality, and we can feel wrong or bad as a result. We are really distressed about what our peer said about the sneakers and can't understand why we are being told not to be upset about it. This will consequently feed into feelings of shame.

In addition to our emotional needs, if our physical needs aren't met, we can develop a belief that we are unworthy of basic physical care, which could very likely manifest through self-destructive behaviours.

Another way of looking at it is that when you are a child, your parents and your upbringing give you a lot of baggage. What you should think, what you should believe, what newspapers you should read, who you should vote for, etc. These aren't things you have much choice about since you haven't had enough time on this earth to decide yourself. Therefore, you learn all this from your family, their belief systems and their projections. Similarly, your parents' shame travels down to you, such as their shame about finances or sex. This is what we call transgenerational shame.

I want to give you an example of shame and the transgenerational element to it.

I have a close friend whose grandfather was killed in World War I. As a result, his family, who were agricultural workers, had no money. My friend's father therefore had very little access to education, and he had to walk barefoot for three miles (5km) every day to school. However, because he was very bright, he managed to get a scholarship to Cambridge.

Surprisingly, his family turned their backs on him because of the baggage they carried. The reaction to his excitement of getting accepted was "Who are you to go to Cambridge? Who do you think you are?"

He did end up going but, once he got there, he was shamed there too because he was different. He was from a family of agricultural workers from Northampton and not from a wealthy family.

My friend's father's shame was then passed down to my friend, and this led to him engaging in addictive, self-destructive behaviours until he finally found his way into recovery in his 30s. Letting go of shame is hard, but it's possible. The first step toward finding freedom from it is to recognize it. Throughout the book we are going to look at how we can do that, and how we might make positive changes.

Nature, Nurture and Needs

Everyone's needs are different and can be impacted by how we are wired genetically. There are plenty of examples whereby two siblings are brought up in the same household, with the same parents, same dynamic, same school experience, etc., but one ends up struggling with an addiction due to low self-worth and negative belief systems while the other does not.

The difference here lies in their emotional needs. One child might need more emotionally – for example, to be told they're good enough by their parents or to be hugged more. The other child might be more independent and need fewer words of validation. Perhaps even less overt signs of care or love.

I definitely needed more attention and words of approval than my younger brother. It has been interesting to see how, even though we had the same upbringing, our needs are not the same and we responded to things in our childhood very differently. I was highly sensitive and, having worked through a lot of my childhood in therapy, can now see that my emotional needs couldn't always be met by my parents. Not because they didn't want to, but because they didn't know how. I can remember feeling very strongly about things, and this wasn't always met with acceptance. Instead, I was told, "Well ... you shouldn't feel like that." I absolutely do not want to demonize my parents, because it wasn't their fault, but I can remember at times being upset or afraid and being told not to worry or that I had "made it up".

REWINDING THE CLOCK

I want you to get your journal back out and turn over onto a clean page. As we have just been talking about childhood and the significance of emotional needs being met, I think it's important for us to go back and access some of the feelings we had as a young child. The purpose of this isn't to demonize caregivers or parents, but simply to identify our own needs and get in touch with our experiences. This helps us validate our experiences and feelings ourselves.

I want you to write a letter to your younger self. Think back to a time that your emotional needs weren't met. A time where you felt scared or sad about something. How did your caregivers respond? Can you remember your caregivers being present, or do you remember spending a lot of time alone?

It doesn't matter what age you are writing to; it could be over a period of time. What would you tell your younger self? How would you try to make them feel safe? Try to remind yourself you were never alone, but that all your fears and feelings were valid.

If you can't quite connect to your younger self, it can help to think of a young member of your family. A niece or nephew perhaps. Be kind to yourself during this process – there is no right or wrong way to write this. Sometimes I find just starting with "Dear (your name)" on a blank piece of paper means that I can write without a filter. It doesn't have to make sense to anyone but you.

Shame and Secrets

What probably doesn't help with the taboo of addiction is that a lot of addictive behaviours happen in secret. Those engaging in addictive behaviours are not likely to go shouting about it. In a previous survey I did on addiction, many of the participants wanted to answer the questions anonymously. Even though they do not necessarily identify as addicts, they aren't proud of their self-destructive tendencies.

There is, of course, a plus side to the secrecy. If no one knows about the destructive behaviours of an addict, then they can keep acting out. There is an element of control that we feel if we are the only ones who know about our addictive behaviours. If our lives seem out of control and we have a lot going on, it seems somewhat comforting that we have our own little secret that no one else can touch or change.

With regards to my eating disorder, it manifested by not being able to eat in public. I would go out for friends' birthday dinners and lie about the fact I couldn't eat with them. My life revolved around how I could get away with not eating, and if I achieved it, I saw this as a victory. It felt like my dirty little secret that nobody knew anything about, something that was mine, something that no one could take away from me. These thoughts and behaviours would isolate me from any social occasion with friends and family, and my life became very insular. This isolation made my eating disorder stronger as it became the only voice I trusted to make me feel good about myself.

There is an expression in Alcoholics Anonymous: "Secrets keep you sick." When it comes to addiction, this is very much the case. Addictive behaviours can manifest because we are acting from a place of shame, self-loathing or feeling worthless. Not only do we keep our behaviour secret, but also the feelings that occur as a consequence. If we were to talk about how we feel to others, we may have to talk about our addiction. This might force us to admit the addiction is real and something we might have to face. The problem is, until we step out of the secretive cycle, we can be stuck in it for many years. This is an extremely painful place to be as we feel very much alone, like no one else knows what we are going through and there is something wrong with us.

If we look at alcoholism or drug addiction, this can manifest as secret drinking or using at home alone. With eating disorders, you could be secretly binging or skipping meals. With an addiction to social media, you could be having dinner with friends but going to the bathroom to secretly check your phone.

For me, the most painful moments of my active addiction were when I was binging/overeating. I was eating in secret because I felt disgusting and because starving myself was no longer working. Food was the only thing that would numb me after a day at work. I would sit in my bed, turn off my phone, put on Netflix and binge.

The self-loathing at this point was probably the worst, but because I wasn't skinny anymore or looking unhealthy, everyone would say I looked great and would express how they were proud of my progress. I felt angry because they didn't think I needed help. People associated my eating disorder with being thin, but eating disorders can manifest in ways not visible to others.

We find it hard to see addiction as an illness since we can't pinpoint the source of the problem with medical scans and tests. This elusiveness is what makes addiction so hard for us to understand and therefore accept.

However, addiction has been with us since the dawn of civilization and possibly even before that. Our relationship with it is complex and is a result of a whole multitude of factors. It is a result of our nature and nurture. It is derived from the DNA we receive from our parents but also the way they brought us up, their belief systems and their shame. This is why delving into your childhood experiences can be a critical step in moving forward with your recovery.

CHAPTER 2
THE MANY THINGS WE CAN BE ADDICTED TO

The Different Types of Addiction

Our brains want us to seek out nice things. If we weren't driven to find food, have sex or find time to relax, we wouldn't have got very far as a species. We would either have starved or not have had any children in the first place! However, in modern society a lot of people have access to a lot of stimulating activities, from drugs to games, from receiving likes to placing a bet.[1]

When I tell my clients that addiction is looking externally to help how we feel internally, they often respond, "But I've got to do *something* to relax, right?" And that is true. Leisure activities are of course encouraged but, as we discussed, they shouldn't negatively impact our lives or make them unmanageable. This can extend beyond drugs to activities that are considered acceptable in our society.

To illustrate this further, we will look at the different types of addiction and how they may manifest. While most of us can easily put alcohol and drugs into the camp of addiction, there are other addictive behaviours that might not be obvious to you, such as reading romance novels! We can be addicted to pretty much anything external – as a fellow in recovery once said to me, "I could pick up anything and use it." As a result, I will not be able to cover every addiction here, but through these examples I hope you will pick up on some common themes. The reality is that it doesn't matter what it is, but what is driving it.

What you are addicted to can also change. Have you ever been to a fairground or arcade and played whack-a-mole? You have a hammer, little moles pop up at different locations and your goal is to hit each mole as fast as you can when it appears. Once you've whacked one mole, a different mole will appear at a different place on the board. You whack the moles down as fast as you can, but they keep popping up despite how many times you whack them down.

This game is a very good way of describing what addiction can be like. Once you address one addictive behaviour, another behaviour – perhaps totally unrelated – will pop up elsewhere. Why? Because underneath the behaviours, you are still trying to control or escape from your underlying feelings. You haven't really looked at the core reasons behind your addictive behaviours. Once you feel like you have one addiction under control, your addiction will pop up in another area of your life, sometimes subtly at first.

This was how my addiction manifested for me. I started using food to change the way I felt when I was 14. This was the first time I engaged in a self-destructive behaviour; it was the beginning of my eating disorder.

Being a teenager was hard, and I massively struggled with my identity. I remember when I first started to restrict my food, I suddenly felt like I had more power over my life. I was at an all-girls boarding school where I compared myself to everyone else's body shape. I hit puberty quicker than the other girls and as a result was always much bigger and taller. This made me feel different. I felt the need to be thin and thought this would lead to me fitting in better. Restricting my food gave me a sense of feeling in control and a sense of purpose.

After a few years, just like whack-a-mole, my addictive tendencies started to manifest as an alcohol problem. I had been threatened with hospitals if I didn't gain weight, and so, against my will, I gained the weight. However, I remember feeling helpless and stuck in a self-loathing spiral. Overwhelmed by feelings of insecurity and sadness and a sense of being different, I started drinking to numb it all out. Following that, my addiction found another way to manifest itself after the age of 20. I discovered drugs. This sped up the process to me hitting my rock bottom and seeking help. Thanks to a period of both inpatient and outpatient rehab, I got clean from drugs and alcohol in my early 20s. However, this didn't mean my eating disorder had gone away. If anything, it was just hiding behind the curtain waiting to pounce at the right time. When I came out of treatment, my eating disorder – my first addiction and what we call "primary" addiction – came back in full force.

My eating disorder wasn't just restrictive. It took all different forms: binging, purging and exercise addiction. I struggled with codependency and became addicted to social media. As you can see, I have been through the spectrum of addictive behaviours and back again.

You may have brushed over the fact that I was addicted to social media. Not everyone drinks alcohol or uses drugs. But we all use social media. What's the harm if everyone else is using it?

I have a client, A, a young female who, when she first came to see me, would never have called herself an addict. She didn't understand why her levels of anxiety were so high, and she wanted help with managing her work–life balance. It was only when we started to look at her relationship to her phone that we started to dig a little deeper and learn what was causing her anxiety.

Every night, when she got home from work, she would be scrolling on her phone before she even knew it. She realized that she got a huge sense of gratification from others when she posted on Instagram. When she had a bad day at work, she would automatically post something on Instagram to feel better. Sometimes she would post a photo of herself that she, the next day, thought she didn't want to share. She found herself having to delete Instagram from her phone every night to avoid her scrolling the next day. She would even find herself being awake hours later than she had planned.

After a few days of no Instagram, she noticed a new pattern emerging. She began constantly checking the news – what we then called doom scrolling. We realized that the constantly changing updates on the news would give her a hit of adrenaline. I asked her how she felt when she was scrolling through the news, and she said angry. So why did she want to consciously click on something that made her angry? I asked her how she would feel if she didn't scroll.

"Bored … Lonely, I guess? I feel stressed and a bit deflated knowing I have to go back to work the next day."

Being angry at the news and concentrating on other people's problems seemed preferable to dealing with her own. The scrolling numbed her from her loneliness. The news headlines gave her something else to focus on and distracted her from the negative feelings she had about her job and the realization that she probably needed to make the difficult decision to change careers.

If we can be addicted to the news, what other types of behaviours are we addicted to that perhaps we're not even aware of?

In the diagram opposite, I've outlined things we can be addicted to and grouped them into categories. You might not have heard of all of these as addictive behaviours before, but I'll elaborate on some of them in the following pages to give you a clearer picture of how they can impact our lives.

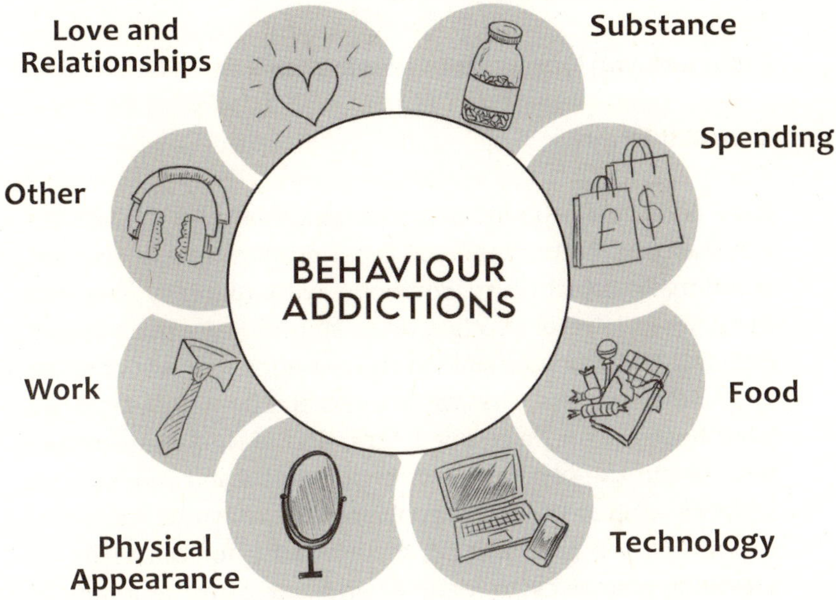

- **Love and Relationships:** Love, codependency, sex, pornography, masturbation
- **Substance:** Alcohol, drugs, nicotine, prescription drugs
- **Spending:** Debt, shopping, online shopping, gambling
- **Food:** Caffeine, sugar, restriction, overeating, binging, purging
- **Technology:** Gaming, social media, phone, news, online browsing, television
- **Physical Appearance:** Plastic surgery, tanning, body dysmorphia, exercise, piercings, tattoos
- **Work:** Workaholism
- **Other:** Collecting/hoarding, music, reading, etc.

Love and Relationships

Let's start with looking more closely at love and relationships.

Love Addiction

Love addiction is about using someone else to change the way we feel. The other person is our drug. Have you ever felt emotionally attached to someone without really knowing them? Have you ever struggled to be alone but also really feared intimacy and commitment? With love addiction, we confuse love with neediness, physical and sexual attraction, pity or the need to rescue or be rescued. Love addiction also means we tend to put the other person on a pedestal and can become seriously distracted and immobilized by romantic fantasies. Essentially, we are avoiding responsibility for ourselves by attaching ourselves to people who are often emotionally unavailable. This becomes extremely painful but, fear not, it can be changed. The first step is changing our behaviours.

Let me give you an example: my client N is a male in his early 40s. He came to me to explore why he hadn't been able to find a stable relationship. This was causing him to feel low and unlovable. During his previous marriage, which ended a few years previously, everything he did and felt had been dictated by his wife. When she was stressed and having a bad day, it then took over his day. He felt helpless to the fact that he couldn't help her and change the way she felt.

Eventually, when the marriage ended, he blamed himself for not being able to meet her needs. This example is typical of a codependent relationship.

I reminded him this was not totally his responsibility. Of course, marriage is a partnership, and most of us want to make our spouse happy. However, we cannot control how people feel. We can support them through challenges in their life, but if someone has a bad day at work, we probably cannot remove the associated stress and anger they're experiencing.

When he started dating again after his marriage, he noticed a pattern starting to emerge. He felt himself getting emotionally attached very quickly to women that he had just met for the first time. When one relationship didn't work out, even after just a week, he would feel deeply distraught, abandoned and rejected. This would ruin his week and make him so anxious that he couldn't eat or sleep. He would have panic attacks and intrusive thoughts that he was going to die alone. As a consequence of all these feelings, he would jump straight back onto the dating apps to find someone else to go on a date with. He wanted to distract himself from the previous person that had left him feeling distraught.

He realized that it wasn't actually about the person he was dating, but about how he felt about himself. His low self-worth was driving him to seek external validation from women. With each new woman he was meeting, he was assigning them with magical qualities and putting them on a pedestal. No matter who they were, they immediately had the ability to change the way he felt and had the power to "save" him from his misery. If they liked him or showed interest in him it showed he was good enough.

We looked at these behaviours, and once he started to develop more awareness around how these patterns were manifesting, we explored what it would look like to abstain from these behaviours. What could he do differently so that he didn't fall back into the same cycle? Once we identified this, we were able to look more closely at his self-worth and build his confidence from within himself rather than externally.

Here are some characteristics of love addiction:

- Becoming emotionally attached without truly knowing someone
- Getting seriously distracted by romantic fantasies
- Struggling to maintain healthy boundaries
- Assigning magical qualities to others and put them on a pedestal

- Struggling to be alone but also fearing intimacy and commitment
- Fearing loneliness and abandonment and therefore staying in destructive relationships, which alienate you from yourself and your friends

Codependency

Codependency is, in its simplest form, "I am only okay if they are okay." It is an addiction to people or people pleasing to get your needs met. So, if my friend, partner or family member is feeling sad or is struggling, I am not okay. If someone is upset with me for whatever reason, I am not okay. If someone is angry about issues unrelated to me, I am not okay.

Codependency usually goes hand in hand with love addiction. Coming from a place of low self-worth, codependency means a person may feel unlovable or unworthy outside the context of their relationships. They depend on the opinions of others to give them a feeling of validation and self-worth. Being highly focused on someone else's needs is a very good distraction from ourselves. Like my client who focused too much on the news, if we are only ever thinking about what the other person needs, we are never asking ourselves what we need. True intimacy is mainly formed when both people expose all the vulnerable parts of themselves and meet each other's needs equally. Therefore, a codependent relationship often lacks true intimacy.

Here are some characteristics of codependency:

- Feeling rejected or upset if someone sets boundaries with you
- Feeling the need to meet your partner's or friend's needs for fear that they might leave
- Being unable to set boundaries or declare your needs in a relationship
- Making yourself responsible for the needs of others

- Attempting to control others
- Manipulating others into taking care of us

Technology

Today, we are more and more likely to spend our time glued to a phone, laptop or iPad. Especially after years of COVID-19, during which we were all stuck at home with our technological devices. Most young people between the ages of 8 and 18 spend around seven and a half hours in front of a screen for entertainment alone.[2]

As an experiment one day, just walk around your local street and notice how many people are looking down rather than up. I find it fascinating but also frightening. Most people are glued to their phone, totally unaware of what is going on around them. Make no mistake, I am also responsible for this at times and have to force myself to put my phone in my pocket or on airplane mode when I go for my morning walks.

Gaming Addiction

Let's start with gaming addiction – it is estimated that 3–4 per cent of gamers globally are addicted to video games, amounting to around 60 million people. In fact, the World Health Organization (WHO) recently classified video game addiction as a mental health disorder.[3]

Gaming addiction is another form of escapism. You can be whoever you want to be, look however you want to look and do things you might not be able to do in the real world. I had a client, a lawyer, who would often use video games to take his mind off stresses at work. After a long day of worry and anxiety, he found the process of breaking blocks on *Minecraft* calming, allowing him to park his anxiety until the next day. He would volunteer to do the "menial tasks" such as gathering resources while other players would build and create.

As with all addictions, gaming can cause neglect of real-world responsibilities. On a weekend, this same client would often play with his phone out of reach and not reply to text messages from friends or family.

Addiction to games, with their in-game purchases, can have financial implications too. Games encourage this by allowing the purchase of "loot boxes" where gamers pay money for the chance to unlock a rare item. A study found that out of the top-100-grossing games in the Google Play and Apple App Stores, 58 per cent and 59 per cent respectively contained loot boxes.[4] There have been reports of people paying hundreds and thousands of pounds on this form of gambling.[5]

Here are some characteristics of gaming addiction:[6] [7] [8]

- Lack of control over time spent gaming
- Preoccupation with gaming, including thinking or fantasizing about it when not playing, or feeling sad, anxious, irritable or angry If stopped from playing
- Lying or hiding game use
- Loss of interest in other activities or not seeing family or friends
- Using games as an escape from the real world
- Playing despite negative consequences such as hand or eye pain, losing a job, declining grades or reduced health or hygiene

Social Media Addiction

Similar to gaming, social media has become a worldwide pastime. An example of this is TikTok, a platform that I myself find quite addictive.

TikTok was released in 2016 and now has over one billion active users monthly, making it one of the biggest social media platforms after Facebook, YouTube and Instagram.

For those of you that have never used TikTok, essentially it is a video-sharing app that allows users to share short, clipped videos that can be as creative as you like, with background music, special effects, stickers and voiceovers.

These short bursts of video play into people's craving for micro-entertainment and video distraction. They provide instant gratification and can also trigger the dopamine response in the brain, leading us to want more and more content. It is easy to spend hours on the app, constantly chasing the dopamine high.

Just like Facebook, YouTube and Instagram, TikTok also has the function of giving and receiving "likes" on posted content. A 2020 study even found similarities between giving likes to content on social media and the giving of gifts.[9] So for both giving and receiving likes, clicking the like button allows instant gratification which drives habitual use and positive reinforcement.

Here are some characteristics of social media addiction:

- Having an uncontrollable urge to go onto your social media
- Completely losing track of time and neglecting your responsibilities
- Deleting social media apps then redownloading them straight away
- Removing yourself from a social occasion to secretly go check your social media
- Devoting so much time to your social media account that it impacts other areas of your life

Work

Working hard is seen as a good thing. At school we are encouraged to study hard, and we are supposed to apply ourselves at work. Slogans such as "Put your mind to something, and you can achieve anything" are commonplace. Now, working hard isn't necessarily a bad thing. However, cell phones that put work emails into our pockets, increased competition in the job market and decreased job security have made work–life balance more and more difficult to manage.

Workaholism is one of the most common addictions, affecting 10 per cent of adults in the United States and 20.8 per cent in France.[10] However, it is important to make the distinction between working due to financial need and working because of a compulsion. This compulsion can be driven by the need for an identity built around achievement or a need to be in control of our lives. Other driving factors include perfectionism, neuroticism, narcissism, low self-esteem or a feeling of incompetence.

I think the easiest way of determining work addiction is by using the Bergen Work Addiction Scale developed by Dr Cecilie Schou Andreassen.[11]

Score yourself out of 5 (1=Never, 2=Rarely, 3=Sometimes 4=Often, 5=Always) for each question:

1 You think of how you can free up more time to work.
2 You spend much more time working than initially intended.
3 You work to reduce feelings of guilt, anxiety, helplessness and depression.
4 You have been told by others to cut down on work without listening to them.
5 You become stressed if you are prohibited from working.
6 You deprioritize hobbies, leisure activities and exercise because of your work.
7 You work so much that it has negatively influenced your health.

It is important to note that this was based on Norwegian employees and so may not reflect other cultures, but Dr Andreassen's study suggested that scoring "often" or "always" four out of the seven times may suggest workaholism. However, even if you scored low, this scale may offer insight into what exactly constitutes work addiction.

Spending

Gambling Addiction

Public Health England's "Gambling-related harms evidence review"[12] defined gambling as playing a game of chance for a prize, betting or participating in a lottery. The review found that in 2018, 54 per cent of the adult population in the UK gambled, 40 per cent if you exclude the National Lottery. The National Lottery was the most common type of gambling, apart from in younger people, with whom scratch cards were more popular.

Advertising from betting companies is commonplace, offering free bets or your money back if x or y happens. Not only this, but smartphones have put 24-hour access to gambling in our pockets. The same Public Health England report found that from 2012 to 2018, the number of people gambling online rose by 50 per cent.

The review also found that 0.5 per cent of the population had a problem with gambling, but a YouGov survey reported the problem is much higher, at 2.7 per cent (roughly 1.4 million people).[13] However, the Public Health England report also found that 3.8 per cent of the population were gambling at "elevated risks", meaning they may experience negative consequences. These people were more likely to gamble online, play casino and bingo games, play electronic gambling machines in bookmakers as well as participate in sports gambling and dog racing.

Other factors making people more likely to participate in problem gambling include: having a family member who has a gambling problem, being more impulsive, being male, experiencing depression, stress and anxiety, participating in longer or a higher number of gambling activities, and drinking alcohol or using other substances.[14 15]

The following Problem Gambling Severity Index (PGSI) was developed as a screen for gambling addiction in Canada but has been used in the Health Survey for England, the Scottish Health Survey and the Welsh Problem Gambling Survey.[16 17]

Answer these questions to see if you or a loved one show signs of gambling addiction:

1 Do you bet more than you can afford to lose?
2 Do you need to gamble with larger amounts of money to get the same feeling?
3 Have you tried to win back money you have lost (chasing losses)?
4 Have you borrowed money or sold anything to get money to gamble?
5 Have you wondered whether you have a problem with gambling?
6 Has your gambling caused you any health problems, including feelings of stress or anxiety?
7 Have other people criticized your betting or told you that you had a problem with gambling (regardless of whether or not you thought it was true)?
8 Has your gambling caused any financial problems for you or your household?
9 Have you ever felt guilty about the way you gamble or what happens when you gamble?

Score 0 for each time you answer "never".

Score 1 for each time you answer "sometimes".

Score 2 for each time you answer "most of the time".

Score 3 for each time you answer "almost always".

If your total score is 8 or higher, you or those closest to you are likely to be experiencing gambling-related harms.

If your total score is between 1 and 7, gambling might still be having a negative impact on your life.[18]

Shopping Addiction

We all need to shop. Buying and selling is something that modern society is based on. However, shopping is more than just buying what we need; it is also a recognized form of entertainment. You can't go to the cinema, watch television, go online or walk down the road without seeing an advertisement telling you to buy this or use that. Large shopping centres or malls have become destinations in themselves, and shopping trips with the girls, such as those in *Sex and the City*, are seen as glamorous and exciting.

Shopping addiction, or compulsive buying, occurs when we start to buy uncontrollably, impulsively and overbudget. While others may buy for the sake of needing an item, people with spending addictions become preoccupied with shopping and often buy to improve their mood, reduce stress, improve their self-image or receive social recognition. In one study, compulsive shoppers reported a sense of power, a sense of having something new or being distracted from other problems.[19]

There is usually an excitement we feel in the lead-up to buying and a sense of relief or a rush when the transaction is happening. However, often after a shopping binge, we may feel regret, guilt and shame about our purchases. This could lead us to hiding or ignoring what we have just bought.[20]

One review looked at studies of 32,000 people from a wide range of countries including the US, Germany, France and Hungary. It estimated around 4.9 per cent of the population were compulsive buyers, and this was higher in university students, at 8.3 per cent.[21]

Shopping addiction is more likely to affect people in their late teens or early twenties, but it can affect older adults too. Some studies, but not all, suggest it is more common in women. Like gambling addiction, people with spending addiction are more likely to suffer from low mood, anxiety and impulsivity, and they may also use addictive substances.

They can also suffer from low self-esteem and feelings of loneliness.

Here are some characteristics of spending addiction:

- Impulsively buying things you do not need, haven't planned to buy or have not budgeted for
- Feeling a rush of anticipation when shopping and a feeling of gratification or excitement when you make the purchase
- Finding yourself feeling guilty after shopping and/or hiding what you've bought
- Buying things to make yourself feel better, relieve stress, or distract yourself
- Being preoccupied with shopping when not actively doing so

Physical Appearance

Modern society, media and the fashion industry all place a lot of importance on how we look. The British Attitudes Survey in 2014 found that 47 per cent of adults agreed that "How you look affects what you can achieve in life", and 32 per cent felt that "Your value as a person depends on how you look".[22] One of the leading causes of unhappiness in young people is their appearance, and another survey by the Mental Health Foundation found that 34 per cent and 35 per cent of teenagers felt anxious and depressed about their body image respectively.[23]

Approximately 0.7–2.4 per cent of the population suffer from a condition called Body Dysmorphia Disorder (BDD). Although it might be slightly more common in women, it affects men too.[24]

This is defined by the Diagnostic and Statistical Manual of Mental Disorders (DSM) as:[25]

A: Preoccupation with one or more perceived defects or flaws in physical appearance that are not observable or appear slight to others. The most common areas people may focus on are their skin (such as acne), hair (going bald or having too much hair) or nose. However, people can become preoccupied with any part of their body.

B: At some point during the disorder, the individual has performed repetitive behaviours (e.g., mirror checking, excessive grooming, skin picking, reassurance seeking) or mental acts (e.g., comparing his or her appearance with that of others) in response to the appearance concerns. Around 40 per cent of those with BDD think about their perceived flaws between three to eight hours a day, and 25 per cent for more than eight hours. These thoughts are intrusive and very distressing.

C: The preoccupation causes clinically significant distress or impairment in social, occupational or other areas of functioning. In a sample of 200 people, 36 per cent did not work for one week in the previous month due to their disorder. People with BDD often have depression, and suicidal thoughts and/or attempts are much higher than in the rest of the population. People who suffer from this are more likely to abuse alcohol and drugs.

D: The appearance preoccupation is not better explained by concerns with body fat or weight in an individual whose symptoms meet diagnostic criteria for an eating disorder. There is of course some overlap with eating disorders which are categorized separately. If this is the case, then both conditions can be diagnosed together.

Having this preoccupation does not mean you are vain. Due to its significant impact and health implications, I recommend speaking to a medical professional if you think you may have BDD, and to speak to a doctor, go to the emergency department or call an ambulance if you are feeling suicidal.

Other

You may have seen that in this category I included music, reading and collecting/hoarding and thought, "But these are hobbies, right?" After all, we encourage people to read, and parents often lament that their child doesn't read enough! Having hobbies is normal and healthy. However, these hobbies may become an addiction if they make our lives unmanageable and negatively impact us, but we continue to do them anyway. For example, I would call collecting art an addiction if it puts us in financial difficulty and we cannot stop.

I listen to a podcast called *The Knowledge Project* with Shane Parrish. In an episode called "Between Pleasure and Pain"[26] he interviews Dr Anna Lembke, an American psychiatrist who is chief of the Stanford Addiction Dual Diagnosis Clinic at Stanford University. With all her awareness and work around addiction, she talks about her personal experience and how it manifested through an addiction to romantic novels. After she had her baby, she found that, to self-soothe and de-stress before she went to bed, she would read romance novels. This was a great distraction and helped her fall asleep. After a while she noticed that she couldn't fall asleep without first reading some of her romance book. As time went on, it escalated to the point where she would take the books into work and, in every break, she found herself compelled to read it, even if it was just 10 minutes.

For Dr Lembke, the romance novels had become a way to change how she felt, and was somewhat of a fix.

In summary, enjoyable activities may become addictions if we use them to cope with negative emotions and continue despite harmful consequences.

SELF-REFLECTION

Now, I know I have just thrown a ton of information at you, some of which you might relate to, some of which you might have seen for the first time. So now I just want you to turn inward for a moment. Looking at all these addictive behaviours, did you identify with any of them?

Using your journal or piece of paper again, jot down which of the addictive categories you think you might fall into, then think about whether you have ever engaged in any of the behaviours in an unloving or self-destructive way. How might your behaviour be self-destructive?

Do you feel that you use these behaviours to distract yourself?

Do you criticize yourself once you've engaged in a specific behaviour? For example, after you have been scrolling online for a few hours, do you beat yourself up for not using that time constructively?

Similarly, did you previously engage in something that you are glad you stopped? Did you notice that something else came in to fill that void?

If you identified with any of the above behaviours, keep them in mind for future exercises as we will explore the feelings around them and how they manifest.

Why Do We Gravitate Toward Certain Types of Addiction?

Addictions such as substance abuse, gambling and shopping are associated with low mood and anxiety. Of course, it's difficult to tell whether the addiction caused the low mood or vice versa. However, the pattern that I see with my clients is that people use these behaviours to distract themselves from how they are feeling inside.

That said, with all the different stimuli out in the world today, is there a reason why someone may be more likely to be addicted to one thing rather than another?

Our perspectives, the thoughts in our minds, the parts we like about ourselves, the parts we don't like, who we want to be and who we think we should be are all part of what I call our intrapsychic landscape. As we have seen, this is based on our personalities and is a consequence of our nature (our DNA) and nurture (our upbringing and external circumstances). The likelihood of engaging in certain addictive behaviours will be influenced by our unique viewpoint on the behaviours themselves. These include:

- Spending addiction is more common in wealthier, market-based economies where shopping is considered an enjoyable leisure activity.[27]
- Low self-esteem is found in workaholism where people may feel a sense of achievement or value in their occupation.
- It might be that you had a lot of exposure to a behaviour when you were younger. Perhaps your parents drank a lot or put you in front of a screen to give them a bit of peace and quiet.

In *Personality Traits and Drug Consumption*, Elaine Fehrman and Dr Vince Egan analysed data from 1,855 respondents regarding 18 different psychoactive substances. They concluded that those more likely to be addicted to substances may have different personality traits to those who are less likely. For example, they found that people who are more likely to use drugs had higher neuroticism and are more open to experiences. The book also shed light on why different people might be more addicted to different substances. For example, they found heroin users seemed to be less extroverted and less agreeable than ecstasy users.[28]

In the same vein, former Harvard professor Edward Khantzian posited his self-medication hypothesis. He felt that three factors interact with each other to make someone reach for a particular substance:

1. The main effect of the drug
2. The person's personality
3. Their psychological suffering

He observed that people with substance misuse had difficulty with their feelings, either being overwhelmed by them or not being able to feel at all. They used substances to relieve the pain they were suffering, experience emotion or control what they were feeling. For example, he described opiates (such as heroin) as reducing feelings of rage.[29]

Therefore, we tend to gravitate toward drugs and behaviours that medicate the unique pain of our landscape. Take my cocaine use as an example:

1. **Main effect of the drug:** It gave me more self-confidence, it made me more social, I was accepted by my friends
2. **My personality:** I am impulsive, I was not conscientious, I was open to trying new things
3. **My psychological suffering:** I was low in mood, I felt worthless, I felt socially anxious, I felt I wasn't an interesting person, I felt lonely

You can see that cocaine helped my psychological suffering. It scratched the itch of my need for acceptance, to join in and to help me with my anxiety.

We've seen that addiction can take many forms. It isn't just about using an illegal substance. Furthermore, what we are addicted to can change depending on our environment and our needs. I don't want you to feel helpless because of this. Rather, I want to help you cultivate more awareness around behaviours that are harmless in themselves but can become problematic when used to take you away from yourself and your feelings. It is a natural human urge to feel good, and as such these wants and desires will never completely leave us. But that is okay. I can certainly still engage in potentially addictive behaviours – sometimes it's exercise, sometimes it's social media and sometimes it's shopping. But the difference now is that because I am more aware of my relationship with the behaviour, I can catch myself in the cycle before it's too late. This self-reflection not only stops me from going too far with a certain behaviour, it also helps me understand how I'm feeling and what I really need at that moment in time. Recovery is a journey, with ups and downs. Sometimes the thoughts or desires to engage with addictive behaviours will be stronger; sometimes they are easier to overcome. However, with time and with the tools I will introduce you to, they will hopefully become more manageable.

As you have seen from this chapter, the substances and/or behaviours come with perceived benefits – either numbing of stress, putting the plaster/band-aid on psychological suffering or the heightening of a high. In the next chapter, we'll explore these perceived benefits and why we begin to use them in the first place.

CHAPTER 3
SEARCHING FOR THE HIGHS

The Highs of Addiction

I think most of us are familiar with the expression "getting high". Most of us have at least a basic understanding of the highs that are associated with substances such as cocaine or heroin. But beyond these drug highs, I would argue that highs also include what we perceive as the benefits of our behaviours. The highs might also look different for everyone – for some it can be an intense high, for others it might be more of a low-level buzz, numbness or sense of escapism.

Many clients who come to see me start off by saying, "I know I drink too much, but I don't want you to challenge my alcohol consumption", or "I know that the amount of exercise I do isn't necessarily healthy, but I don't want to change that just yet". So why do they keep engaging in these behaviours if they know they aren't serving them in a healthy way? Well, because it feels good!

Now I want to look more closely at the highs our addictive behaviours may give us. There must be a reason we engage in these behaviours, right? Firstly, I think we need to be realistic about them. More importantly, if we understand the need that our addictive behaviour satisfies, then it can help us understand where the need comes from. Following this, we can replace that addictive behaviour with a healthier alternative, be it a hobby, mindfulness or exploring our needs through therapy.

Let's look at my personal example of Khantzian's self-medication hypothesis in the previous chapter. Cocaine made me more confident and made me fit into a certain social circle. Through this lens, I can understand my needs of having more self-confidence and fitting in. This can give me something to focus on with a therapist, or I can try another hobby, such as yoga, to meet new people and build healthier connections there. Don't worry, we will look at how we change our behaviour patterns later on.

But, before we go any further, I need to tell you some of the sciencey stuff. More and more research is being conducted to understand what happens in our brains with regards to addiction. One thing we do know is we have been wired to focus on the highs for thousands of years.

The Sciencey Stuff

It is natural that we want to do things that make us feel good or rewarded. Animals do this too! When we train a dog to sit or to give us their paw, we use treats as a reward. These pleasurable feelings give them positive reinforcement which makes them more likely to repeat that behaviour. The desire to eat, drink and have sex means that we can survive as a species.

But how exactly do we get these pleasurable feelings, and how do our brains help us remember how to get them again? If we understand this, then it will give us a good foundation for understanding why we become programmed to seek these highs. We call the part of the brain that does this the reward pathway, or mesolimbic system.

To put it very simply, there are three main areas of the brain that are involved: the **prefrontal cortex**, the **nucleus accumbens** and the **ventral tegmental area** (VTA).[1]

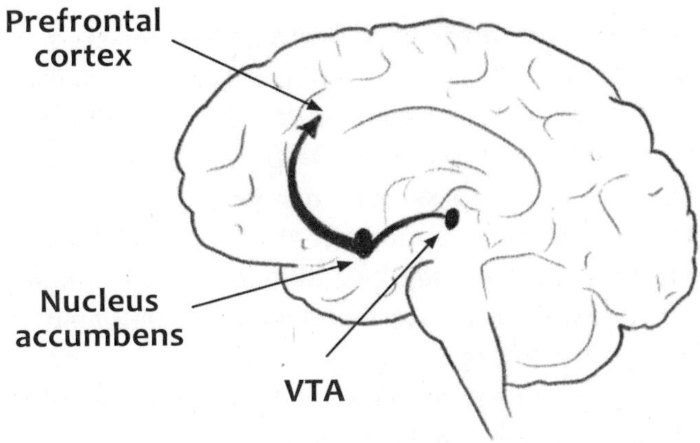

1 **The prefrontal cortex:** This is the area involved in thinking our thoughts. It can help us weigh up any conflicting views we have and decide what action to take. It helps us judge what is good and what might be bad, suppress our basic urges and consider the future consequences of actions.
2 **The nucleus accumbens:** This is the area of the brain that processes the idea of reward and motivation. It is connected to other parts of the brain called the amygdala and the hippocampus which are involved in emotions and memory respectively.
3 **The ventral tegmental area (VTA):** The VTA contains the neurotransmitter dopamine, which can be released to both the nucleus accumbens and the prefrontal cortex. It can send information to the prefrontal cortex and the nucleus accumbens through connections called neurons.

When a rewarding stimulus is experienced, such as eating a chocolate cake, dopamine is sent from the VTA to the nucleus accumbens. This then interacts with the amygdala (to give us a nice emotion of happiness or satisfaction) and the hippocampus (to help us remember that we like this food and remind us where we can get it again).

This was discovered using experiments on rats. Rats were given a pleasing electric stimulus to the nucleus accumbens whenever they pressed a button. This resulted in them continually pressing the button to get that nice feeling. They liked this so much that some of the poor rats didn't want to eat anymore, but only wanted to press the button instead.[2 3]

Dopamine is also sent to our prefrontal cortex, which helps us consciously appreciate the chocolate cake and that we have been rewarded by eating it. This will influence our future decisions when we are weighing up between different actions in the future.

So, if we engage in activities that stimulate this reward pathway, our brains will experience a high, give us a positive emotion around that high, remember that the activity gave us a high and make us want to experience that high again – even if, like the rats who kept pressing the button and didn't want to eat, it has negative consequences.

Of course, this is a very simplified explanation about what is going on. But I think it is important to have this basic idea in mind when we think about addictive behaviours and the highs that come with them.

The Different Highs of Different Addictive Behaviours

As we saw, how we perceive addictive behaviours, our reasons for engaging in them and our experience with them vary from person to person. However, there are often some similarities. Let's take a second look at some of the addictive behaviours we were talking about last chapter and explore what their perceived benefits might be. I want you to be mindful and write down your answers to the questions following each section. Try to pinpoint and contemplate any highs or benefits you might recognize in your own experience.

Love and Relationships

Let's start with looking at love and relationships.

Love Addiction

Obviously love and lust are wonderful feelings, and feelings that have helped us survive for thousands of years. These feelings encourage us to be close to one another and even to reproduce. The neurobiological reasons why we fall in love are complex, but the process releases those feel-good chemicals in our brain.

In 2005, a study using functional MRI scans (scans that pick up on brain activity) monitored college students while they looked at pictures of someone special to them. This caused their brains to be active in areas rich with dopamine such as the VTA.[4] Sex and orgasms also release dopamine in the nucleus accumbens.[5] Therefore, some scientists have argued that this is why being in love or having sex can feel like a cocaine rush.[6]

Now, there are a few different types of love. There are the initial feelings of lust, sheer excitement and adrenaline of falling in love with someone new and fantasizing about your life together. Feeling desirable and desiring are also part of that new love. Additionally, there is also the feeling of being in love with a long-time partner. This usually doesn't give us so much of a buzz but more of a sense of belonging, a sense of deep trust and safety. With both types of love, being with our partner or thinking about them can distract us from any stresses or worries in our own life. For example, the excitement of seeing your partner allows you to tolerate a difficult day at work.

I have a client who would jump from one relationship to another looking for that initial buzz – in fact, she couldn't remember a time in the last 25 years when she was on her own. She described the feeling of engaging in a relationship with someone new. "Nothing else matters in that moment," she said. "When I meet someone I have feelings for, suddenly things start to make sense." She would forget about any stresses, problems at work or family issues, and she even found herself more productive at work and in the gym because she felt she had more of a purpose.

However, once the initial buzz began to wear off, she would often realize that she was not compatible with her then partner. They would break up, she would feel even worse about herself and she would worry that she'd never find love. She would then start looking through her dating apps again and the cycle would repeat. By continuously dating, she was reinforcing the idea that her self-worth was reliant on what a new partner thought of her. By chasing this high, she was unable to recognize and cultivate value in herself and be comfortable on her own.

SELF-REFLECTION ON NEW RELATIONSHIPS

Think about how you feel when you are in a new relationship or about to go on a date with someone, and jot down your thoughts. Then, reflect on how you feel about the stressors in your life when this happens.

Codependency

Codependency – the idea that "I'm only okay if they are okay" – often occurs within intimate relationships. But it is more about keeping yourself in a relationship and making it work for the other person, as opposed to going from one relationship to another trying to achieve that "love high".

So why does that feel good? Making sacrifices for their partner means that the codependent feels useful and needed. They feel rewarded every time someone asks them for something, they do it for that person and that person is grateful. The other person relies on them more, which the codependent often interprets as acceptance.

It's worth mentioning that codependency is second nature for us. Just like with love, we have survived through the centuries by looking after and taking care of one another. Codependents are very compassionate, and being compassionate is a great skill to have. When you are empathic, people will trust you more, and it feels good to be able to hold space for someone and make a difference in their life. However, with codependency, it can come at the cost of your own self-worth and achieving true connection.

I had a client who was raised by his grandmother. Even though he knew that this was not his parents' choice, he felt rejected by them. He carried that shame with him and that feeling of unworthiness. He felt that he didn't have many true connections with people and often felt uneasy speaking one-on-one with others. Only in doing favours for people could he experience a connection with them and feel valued. As a result, he was an extremely well liked and respected person, but he lacked true intimacy with other people.

SELF-REFLECTION ON SUPPORT IN RELATIONSHIPS

Think about whether you ever felt useful in a relationship. Have you helped a friend or loved one in need and given them your support? How did that feel? Write down your thoughts in your journal or on a piece of paper.

Technology Addiction

Smartphones and Social Media

Smartphones have undoubtedly changed the way we live our lives. There are an estimated 6.92 billion smartphones used worldwide[7] – so they must be doing something right! They provide us with real-time news and information, bring messaging, games and social media to our fingertips, help us when we are lost and enable us to shop from home.

Social media allows us to keep in contact with friends and family who live out of reach (both geographically and socially), and during COVID-19 apps such as Houseparty and Zoom kept us connected. There are people who have launched their careers on TikTok and YouTube who may have never had the opportunity to do so otherwise. Others have been able to find their voice and share their opinion in a way that they may feel inhibited to in real life. Friendships and marriages have also been started using social media.

Let's look at social media. If we think back to our reward pathway, we also release dopamine after successful social interactions. Some functional imaging studies also suggest that the nucleus accumbens is activated when people expect to receive positive social feedback.[8] Therefore, smartphones and social media provide us with a potentially unlimited supply of positive stimuli. If we get a lot of likes on a post, that affirms us, we feel accepted and we feel connected.

Some social media apps use a kind of gamification to encourage users to keep coming back. For example, on Snapchat in 2015 there was a new feature added called a "snap streak". This is a representation of how many consecutive days you and a specific friend have managed to send a photo or video back and forth. You and your friend must both send a photo or video to each other within a 24-hour period, or your snap streak will revert back to zero. Users compete with other friends to see who can maintain the longest streak as a sign of social status, a symbol of friendship or acceptance, or the general pleasure of achieving a high score.[9]

Similar to social media, scrolling through the news can also give us some benefits. For example, during the initial outbreak of COVID-19, people found themselves scrolling through some rather frightening news stories, but they couldn't stop. Their feelings of uncertainty were soothed by getting answers, no matter how uncomfortable those answers were. Understanding and learning about something can give us a feeling of control over it. Focusing on the news can also be used as a distraction from our own problems in life.[10]

Essentially, smartphones are devices that can give us a hit of dopamine on demand. Through social media likes, gaming or scrolling through news or dating apps, we can distract ourselves from what is going on around us, feel desired, accepted, connected and affirmed. The easy access means we can keep coming back again and again. This is what makes the smartphone so dangerous. We take the smartphone wherever we go – to work, to dinner or even to bed. As a result, we may find ourselves never being truly present in our surroundings or with the people around us. The accessibility of an easy dopamine hit can make it very easy to slip into addictive patterns.

SELF-REFLECTION ON YOUR SOCIAL MEDIA

Think about your social media usage. If you post something on social media, how often do you check how many likes you have? How do you feel if a post does well? Write down your thoughts in your journal or on a piece of paper.

Gaming Addiction

It is easy to see why lots of people play video or computer games. First, most games are designed to be competitive or present a challenge to be overcome. Getting a high score can bring a sense of achievement. Brain scans have shown that playing goal-related games increases the release of dopamine in the nucleus accumbens.[11] Next, computer games can be a way of socializing and spending time with our peers, either together in the same room or online. Through smartphones, games are even more accessible than ever.

Gaming can be a form of escapism where we might be inclined to spend more and more time online as our online persona, where we feel accepted by a like-minded community, and have a dopamine-driven sense of achievement from overcoming virtual challenges. This can come at a cost to our physical health and "real world" responsibilities.

SELF-REFLECTION ON YOUR GAMBLING HABITS

Think about the games you play. What type of games do you like most and where do you play them? What would trigger you into picking up a controller or your smartphone? Write down your thoughts in your journal or on your piece of paper.

Work Addiction

Now let's explore workaholism. Work is, in itself, rewarding. Think about a time that you finished an assignment for school or a project at work that took a lot of effort and many hours of your time. It probably felt great to hand it in. I certainly know what it feels like to get a chapter in on time to my editor – a huge sense of relief and elation.

Work can give us a sense of accomplishment. Productivity gives us purpose, and when we have purpose in our lives, it feels good to get up each morning and work toward a goal.

Workaholics often love the different personas they can be at work. They present a version of themselves to their colleagues – one of high quality and drive – and it gives them a sense of being in control as well as a feeling of being important, respected and recognized. They may experience a rush when closing a deal or completing a successful operation. Workaholism is also more likely to bring financial stability.

In an interview, Dr Gabor Maté talks about the reasons he wanted to become a doctor. Maté had a traumatic upbringing – he was Jewish, born during World War II in Hungary. To protect him, his mother sent him away to be looked after by others in a safer environment, but as a result, Maté felt unwanted his whole life. Although his adult self realizes his mother did this for his own good, as a child, he only saw his mother rejecting him. As he grew older, he said to himself, "What job can you do where people always need you? Well, become a doctor." And this is what gave him the huge sense of purpose and feeling worthy that he had missed his entire life.[12]

Working hard to achieve your goals is obviously a good thing, but working can also be an excuse not to spend time at home, or it can be used to avoid dealing with personal problems or feelings such as believing we are unlovable. As a result, we can spend more time at work where we feel important and useful, and less time dealing with emotional or personal problems.

SELF-REFLECTION ON YOUR WORK LIFE

Think about your attitude to work. How do you feel when you are at work compared to at home? How do you feel if you get praise from either a client or your boss? Write down your thoughts in your journal or on a piece of paper.

Spending Addiction

Gambling Addiction

Let's look at the perceived benefits of gambling. Again, the biochemical incentives and reward pathways are complex, and this is a very simplified explanation. We might assume that the high of gambling revolves around winning and making money. Indeed, one study looking at dopamine release during a slot-machine task found that the amount of dopamine released in the brain seemed to correlate with winning a higher reward.[13] However, it might not be so straightforward.

You may be familiar with the idea of loss-chasing, where those who lose money still want to gamble to regain their losses. One study found that "pathological gamblers" had released higher levels of dopamine than the "healthy controls" when they lost money.[14] This indicated that dopamine release in those that are addicted to gambling doesn't seem to be just about winning money.

It also doesn't account for gamblers who enjoy the process of gambling and are excited by the uncertainty of whether they will win or not. Another study found that rats responded to rewarding stimuli most frequently when they were not sure when they would be rewarded. In other words, the reward didn't always come when they pressed the button but only came every so often.[15] In "pathological gamblers", one study found that the amount of dopamine released is at its highest when the chance of winning or losing is around 50:50, the most uncertain you can be if you will win or not![16] There is a theory that this could be an evolutionary mechanism that helps animals continue to look for food even if past experience tells them the chances of finding it in each area is quite low.[17]

There is also enjoyment in the socializing element of gambling – talking with your friends about upcoming races or sports matches can be exciting and fun, and there are also benefits in terms of keeping your brain engaged.

Being observant and studying patterns and numbers while gambling can sharpen your mind.

Of course, when we become addicted to gambling it can start to get out of control. These days, we don't even have to go out to place bets; it can be done from the comfort of our own homes. A client of mine described coming home from work each day and opening his Bet365 app. He said this would release all the pressures of the day, and he felt like it was his one bit of fun he could access easily. Even when he started to lose money, he found it difficult to stop because of the thrill he would get from the game itself.

SELF-REFLECTION ON YOUR GAMBLING HABITS

Do you gamble? If so, think about how you feel just before you know the result compared to after you have won. When might you place a bet on your smartphone? Where are you when you do this, and what has happened that day? Write down your thoughts in your journal or on a piece of paper.

Shopping Addiction

We've all heard of retail therapy, where we buy something as a treat to make us feel better and give us a sense of control or autonomy.[18] When you really think about it, shopping is like going on the hunt for something and then taking that prize back home. As such, some brain-imaging studies have shown unique changes in people with spending addiction in the part of the brain involved with reward.[19] [20] However, this has yet to fully explain how this causes our normal shopping to become addictive. Shopping with friends can again be a social activity, and owning or wearing the right items can give us a sense of status, achievement or worth.

As with other addictive behaviours, the internet has given us constant access to online shopping. My clients describe a low-level buzz from searching through pages and pages of products, trying to find the perfect pair of shoes or the perfect shirt to finish their outfit. If they find something they like, they feel a thrill around the upcoming delivery. Some may spend hours looking for clothes across a whole range of different websites.

Wearing the most expensive jewellery or driving a nice car is seen as desirable, while buying the latest trend can help us fit in. However, excessive shopping without budgeting can obviously lead to financial consequences.

SELF-REFLECTION ON YOUR SHOPPING HABITS

Do you sometimes indulge in some retail therapy or shop for leisure? If so, think about how you feel when you're browsing and when you make the purchase. How long does that feeling last? Write down your thoughts in your journal or on a piece of paper.

A Personal Note on the Perceived Benefits of Addiction

Now that we know a bit more about different types of highs within some of the different types of addictive behaviours, I want to give you a personal example of the perceived benefits of one of my own addictive behaviours.

I must be careful not to glamorize addiction here, because it is certainly not glamorous, but I do think it is important to talk about what I initially got out of my addiction, as it can help us be realistic about why we get stuck in an eventually destructive cycle. At the beginning we don't know that our behaviour is destructive or can become a form of self-harm.

As I have mentioned previously, my eating disorder was my first addiction. And it developed at a time when I felt most vulnerable and alone. My eating disorder became my friend, the voice in my head that gave me confidence and made me feel like I had achieved something at the end of each day. It was only mine. No one could take it away from me, so in the moments I felt frightened, alone or angry, I always had something to cheer me up, to make me feel in control and proud. Finally, I had found something that helped me feel better about my appearance. The kick I got when someone said, "Oh, you look like you've lost weight", was enormous. I equated thinness with self-worth, so the more weight I lost, the more self-worth I believed I had.

The other high I felt when I was starving was that of high energy and alertness. During the times that I was physically starving, I felt the strongest buzz. This became a double whammy for me – in addition to this physical high, I felt powerful and proud of the fact that I was able to not eat.

Even though engaging with this addictive behaviour didn't end well for me, that's not to say that it was all bad. In fact, when I started to get a better understanding of why I initially engaged in my eating disorder, I understood that it was a protective mechanism for me, a shield if you like. Although this shield was destructive, it did at first provide me relief from emotional stress.

Similarly, drinking initially gave me a sense of newfound confidence. The kind of confidence I had been yearning for my whole life. I had lots of friends at the girls' school I was at, but I rarely got invited to anything outside of it. Basically, I wasn't invited to the parties where the boys were, and I thought this was because there was something wrong with me. I wasn't as pretty, cool or funny as the other girls and so when I was invited to my first "proper party" at the age of 15, and I had my first ever few drinks, the elation I experienced was like nothing I'd felt before – suddenly I could talk to boys! Perhaps like a lot of people who are drinking for the first time, my first experience of alcohol ended badly – I took it too far, threw up and then passed out in the bathroom of my friend's house. But that didn't matter; despite feeling horrendously ill the next morning, I had this excitement and bubbly feeling that I had finally found something that I could rely on to make me feel included.

I am finally at a point in my recovery where I can look back and analyse the benefits these highs gave me. Obviously, I don't underestimate the pain my addiction caused – not just for me, but for my friends and family. But I can pinpoint moments of my drinking or partying and laugh, and doing this with friends in recovery was such a relief. This has been a huge help with being able to forgive myself for some of my behaviours and knowing I am not alone.

Euphoric Recall

It is important that I introduce the phrase euphoric recall here, because it can be a slippery slope when thinking about our past addictive behaviours. When talking with clients who are very early in their recovery, I find it essential to explain to them that, when you are first abstaining from a behaviour, it is common to experience euphoric recall. I want them to be prepared because it can come out of nowhere and feel overwhelming.

Euphoric recall, put very simply, is when we look back at the past with rose-tinted glasses, only remembering the good stuff. It exaggerates the fun times, even if there weren't actually that many, and it fails to acknowledge all the bad that came with them. This kind of thinking can in itself be very addictive, as by thinking of the highs you had, you can experience a release of dopamine. Herein lies the problem. Euphoric recall is a common cause of relapse, especially during the first few months or even years of recovery.

A good example of euphoric recall occurs with love addiction. With this addiction, it is very common to look at someone and assign magical qualities to them, or to simply fantasize about their good qualities. Despite the obvious reasons that a relationship ended, euphoric recall means you can re-experience a filtered version of the "perfect" bits that bears little resemblance to the actual relationship. This can cause real suffering and yearning and can keep you trying to rekindle something with someone that was not right for you in the first place.

It is very common to experience euphoric recall. I certainly did, and it made the beginnings of my recovery that much harder.

So how do you deal with it? Well, I often tell my clients to "play the tape forward". This is essentially when we think about the consequences of our actions before engaging in the behaviour. Let me give you an example.

A few months ago, I was in session with a client who I have been seeing for about three years. She initially came to me for help with her intense panic and anxiety attacks but hadn't acknowledged that her drinking, drug and spending addictions were all playing a part. Her drinking and drug use would lead to endless hours of online shopping, and then she would panic that she had overspent and suffer with extreme anxiety around her finances. She would also drink to blackout and the next day would be messaged by friends telling her how badly she had behaved and how she should be ashamed of herself. That would lead to further anxiety and panic.

We decided to look at abstaining safely from alcohol and drugs as a good starting point for change. After a few months of abstinence, she noticed a huge change in her panic attacks and anxiety. She could now directly link her alcohol and drug use, and the subsequent behaviours, to her attacks. After about six months of abstinence, we were in a session, and she told me about a wedding that she was going to over the summer. It was her best friend's wedding and she really wanted to have a few drinks. Her best friend had always been her drinking buddy, and they'd previously had such good times together talking about when she was going to get married and drinking champagne. She missed the buzz and excitement of her life (here she was experiencing some euphoric recall), even though she was grateful that she didn't feel so panicky all the time.

I asked her to play the tape forward – what would happen if she decided to pick up a drink that day? Well, there were many possible outcomes: maybe she would get really drunk, take drugs and end up back at home on the internet. Maybe she would only have one drink and not go home and excessively shop. Maybe she would have one drink, that would lead to the next, that would lead to blackout, and she wouldn't even remember her best friend's wedding. Either way, after playing the tape forward, she decided that it was too risky. She had worked hard at her abstinence and felt better for it. She understood that she was only recalling the good parts of her drinking, and when she played the tape forward, she remembered that engaging in her addictive behaviours rarely ended positively.

IDENTIFYING YOUR HIGHS

These behaviours serve a purpose. We now know that highs are not necessarily physical euphoric highs but can sometimes manifest as a low-level buzz, a numbness or a sense of escape. They can also bring us out of ourselves and help us access parts of us that we wouldn't be able to otherwise. As humans, it's okay to engage with (some of!) these behaviours because it's only natural when we are stressed to want to unwind. However, finding these behaviours relaxing and numbing might make us inclined to engage in them more and more.

Can you relate to a low-level high? Have you identified with any of the other types of highs we have talked about?

It's worth asking what your life might look like if you didn't engage in these behaviours as often. You wouldn't experience your high as much, but what would that mean? What would that leave space for?

Have you ever found yourself in the middle of something but changed what you were doing to go and get your high?

Jot down your thoughts in your journal or on a piece of paper.

Again, I do not want to glamorize these behaviours, but identifying their benefits can help us understand why we are doing them and thus gain perspective on why they might be difficult to stop.

The problem with chasing these highs is that we are programmed to want more and more. So how do we know when enough is enough? Are we ever satisfied? We'll look at that more closely next.

CHAPTER 4
IS IT EVER ENOUGH?

The Cycle of Addiction

We now know a little more about the highs of addiction and why we might get involved with behaviours or substances in the first place. It's natural to want more of something that feels good, right? Unfortunately, some things are too good to be true and this is the case with addictive behaviours, their benefits and their highs. The problem is we keep wanting more. Engaging in them can be the first stage of being trapped in an addictive cycle.

You might be familiar with this aspect of drug and alcohol addiction: someone who is addicted to a substance will often start to take more and more of it to get the same level of high. What you might not know is that this can be seen in addictive behaviours too. For example, research shows that those with gaming addiction may need more and more complex, time-consuming and difficult challenges to achieve the same sense of satisfaction and immersion.[1]

Once we start, is it ever enough? And what does enough actually mean?

We will start with physical addictions such as drug and alcohol addiction as these are the most researched and widely known. I'll give a simplified background on physical dependence and how our brains' pathways might be altered when we regularly take these substances, which means once we start, we want more. I will go even further and focus on the emotional side of this – the psychological cycle of addiction.

On this line of thinking, if we are using substances to distract us from our feelings and cover the cracks, will they ever be enough to fill it? Well, let's have a look...

Physical Addictions of Tolerance and Dependence

How might our initial use lead to us being trapped in a cycle of addiction? And what is this cycle anyway?

The National Institute on Alcohol Abuse and Alcoholism defines the addiction cycle in three stages:[2]

1. **The Binge/Intoxication Stage**: This is when we take an intoxicating substance, and we get the high that we talked about last chapter. For example, we start drinking alcohol, and this makes us feel drunk.
2. **Withdrawal/Negative Effect Stage**: This is when we start to feel negative feelings when we are not taking the substance. For example, we do not get enjoyment from other activities that do not involve alcohol, and we can get physical withdrawal symptoms.
3. **Preoccupation/Anticipation Stage**: This is when we look to take the substance again after a while without it. For example, we get cravings for alcohol and have an urge to go and buy a drink.

The speed at which we go through this cycle can vary depending on the person and the substance they are taking. Someone might go through it a few times in one day, whereas someone else might go through it over the course of a week or month. For example, nicotine is broken down in the body quite quickly (it has what we call a short half-life), so those with a nicotine addiction will need to smoke again soon after finishing their last cigarette. THC, found in marijuana, has a longer half-life, and thus users typically smoke less frequently. However, as time goes on, these stages tend to get more intense.[3]

Let's go through each stage in more detail.

The Binge/Intoxication Stage

The more times we use a substance and experience a high, the more surges of dopamine (and other chemicals) reinforce the association in our brains between the drug and feeling good. However, our brains also build a relationship between the substance and other cues associated with the drug's use. For example, going to the bar would be a cue associated with drinking alcohol. Over time, this cue of going into a bar can trigger the urge to drink. I knew a client who took ecstasy when he went to a music festival. Even though he got clean many years ago, listening to dance music at a festival was a cue to instantly give him the urge to take it again.

Furthermore, as we keep on taking a substance, our brains are increasingly wired to turn the use of the substance into a habit.

The Withdrawal/Negative Effect Stage

If we continue to take a substance, over time the brain adapts to these surges of dopamine. It does this by toning down the amount of dopamine it releases in future stimulations. Think of it like when we turn down the volume of our headphones when the music is too loud. This has been shown in studies where addicted people, when given a stimulant, were found to release less dopamine than non-addicted controls.[4] Brain-imaging studies have also shown that people with addiction have a lower level of a certain dopamine receptor that can receive the dopamine signals and pass on the pleasurable messages to other areas of the brain.[5] All this means we may need more and more of a substance to get the same level of high we first experienced. We call this becoming tolerant.

On top of this, when the effects of the drug have worn off, there is evidence that the amygdala (the area of the brain that processes emotions) releases chemicals that make us feel stress. We call this withdrawal. These negative emotions can lead us to want to take the substance again. Withdrawal from some substances can also make us feel physically unwell and can be severe.

The Preoccupation/Anticipation Stage

This stage occurs when we begin to seek the substance again after we have stopped taking it for a while. For some people, this could be after only a few hours. This can be called a craving.

We previously talked about the prefrontal cortex helping us make decisions and suppressing our urges. Some scientists talk about there being two parts to it: a "Go" system and a "Stop" system.

The Go system helps us make decisions and initiate actions that allow us to achieve our goals. Research shows that when our brains are triggered by cues, activity in the Go system increases and creates an urge for us to use the substance again. For example, we get the urge to drink alcohol when we go to the bar because our brains remember that we used to get alcohol there. The Go system also seems to activate the habit-forming areas in our brain and contributes to the impulsivity involved in seeking a substance.

The Stop system is involved in ceasing the activity of the Go system. In other words, it tries to put a stop to our habits and reduce the ability for cues to trigger relapse.

When we are at this stage of addiction, our Go system is overactivated, which makes us engage in habit-like substance seeking. Our Stop system is underactivated, which means we are less likely to resist taking the substance.[6]

Breaking the Stages Down Further

We can now see how addictions to substances can start in the brain, and breaking these stages down further into six parts really helped me understand things more clearly.[7] [8]

1 **Initial use**: We first take the substance
2 **Abuse:** We use the substance in a way that is harmful – this could be the first time you take the substance
3 **Tolerance**: We need more and more to get the same level of high
4 **Dependence:** We can get withdrawal symptoms when we do not take the substance, or we do not find pleasure in other activities that do not involve the substance
5 **Addiction**: We continue to use the substance despite it negatively affecting our lives, whether financially, socially or physically
6 **Relapse**: We try to stop but then are triggered to take the substance again

The Psychological Addiction Cycle

We've now seen what happens in our brain; now let's look at how we might experience addiction emotionally. On the next page you'll see a diagram showing the psychological cycle we go through once we are addicted to something.[9] I'll use my alcohol abuse as an example when explaining all five stages of this cycle.

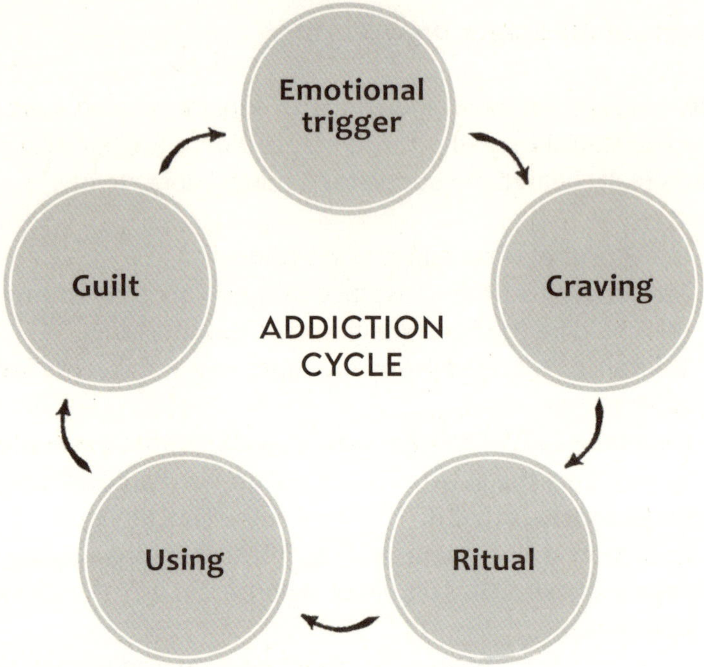

1 **Emotional Trigger**: We experience some sort of negative emotion; either someone says something that hurts us, we feel shame about our using or we simply are having a comedown from the night before. We are unable to avoid these emotions in life, and so we start this repetitive cycle.

Let's take a night out for example – I felt very insecure and didn't like the way I looked. My trigger would be the feeling of immense social anxiety as well as a fear of bumping into someone I had behaved badly with a few weeks prior.

2 **Craving:** We fantasize about using to get rid of the uncomfortable emotion we are feeling. We experience obsessive thoughts around what will happen if we use, and sometimes we even obsess about what would happen if we didn't use … but it gets too much and feels too stressful.

I would imagine the buzz that I would get from drinking, the immediate relief of anxiety and the excitement of not knowing where the night was going to take me.

3 **Ritual:** We start behaving in a way that prepares us for using again. For example, an alcoholic may start stocking up on alcohol before they binge, or someone who smokes starts to roll all their cigarettes before lighting up.[10] [11]

Before the night out, I'd visit a certain friend's house where I felt safe. This friend always had a lot of alcohol for pre-drinks, and we'd egg each other on, take lots of pictures and play music.

4 **Using:** We use again. We lose control, even though we perhaps momentarily feel in control once we have temporary relief from emotions and cravings. We might intend to use only a little bit, just enough to keep the emotions and cravings at bay, but before we know it we have totally lost control.

I would get mind-numbingly drunk before we went to the party, make myself sick and then drink more when we got there.

5 **Guilt:** We feel guilty for behaving in the same way, and the shame cycle continues. We really want to stop the cycle, and we start thinking of ways we can change. But after a while, something happens in our lives that evokes unpleasant feelings, or we are still feeling shame from the way we behaved. These feelings are too much to handle, so we start the cycle again.

The depression, guilt and feelings of "hangxiety" I experienced the morning following a night of using were so severe and painful that I would want to start drinking again just to numb how I was feeling.

Of course, the above stages and cycles are based on substance misuse. But there is some evidence that there are similarities between behavioural and substance addictions on a neurobiological level.[12] [13] Either way, knowing how substance addiction works can give us a background understanding of the addictive cycle.

Behavioural Addictions

So let's take a closer look at addictive behaviours. We have seen that, just as people use substances to help them deal with difficult emotions, shame or day-to-day stresses, they can also use addictive behaviours. One of the problems is that if we keep using certain behaviours to improve the way we feel, the bar will always rise. I describe it to clients as a topless top – it will never be enough.

Let me introduce the phrase "hedonic treadmill", which was coined by Brickman and Campbell.[14] They suggest that although winning the lottery or buying our dream house will make us temporarily happy, we will eventually return to our baseline of happiness. Each time we come home to our new house, the satisfaction we feel will get slightly less until it doesn't bring us that rush of happiness anymore. Our expectations and our aspirations adapt and then align to our new normal.[15] So, in order to get that same feeling, we need a new event or achievement. This can lead us to pursue one pleasure after another.

Let me ask you this: have you ever said to yourself, "When I have this job, I will be happy", or "When I have this much money, I will stop needing to work so hard", or "When I meet the right person, I will feel complete and fulfilled"? What happened when you got these things or achieved what you wanted? Did you feel satisfied? Did you feel like it was enough? Or did you then want more?

Today, we live in a culture where we are always told to want more, do more, buy more. We could argue this has brought benefits to society, but it can also mean that we are never truly satisfied with what we have. More money, more clothes, more followers – our thirst is unquenchable.

However, the quality of our experience changes in response to our exposure to stimuli over time. Does chasing the next dose of happiness and adapting to want more sound familiar?

CAN YOU GET SATISFACTION?

I want you to list a few times in your life when you had a desire for something. Examples include a toy that you really wanted as a child, a new promotion at work or an investment that would give you a lot of profit.

Write out the outcome of these desires in your journal or on a piece of paper. How did you feel when you got what you wanted?

Then I want you to think about how long that happiness, feeling of elation or satisfaction lasted. Can you even remember the feeling you had around it? Was it short-lived, leaving you wanting more? Did you soon start thinking about the next thing you wanted?

Let me give you a common example of chasing the next dose of happiness. Have you ever sat down to watch a TV show with the intention to watch just a couple of episodes? You've had a long, tiring and stressful day at work, so you've been waiting all day to get home to watch your favourite show. Finally you get home, sit down and watch a few episodes. Then you realize that you need to make your dinner. But you don't want to – you want to watch another few episodes, because the last two weren't enough. You thought that the two you had set out to watch were going to scratch your itch and leave you satisfied, but they didn't. Even if you get to the end of the series, do you then feel satisfied? Or do you immediately start looking for the next series to get into?

My Story – It Was Never Enough

I want to now describe my experience with eating disorders to give you a better understanding of how behavioural addictions follow the psychological cycle of addiction.

Whether it was conscious or not, my behaviours were always started by a feeling – an **emotional trigger**. This didn't always have to come from someone else; a lot of the time it was how I felt about myself, or even just how I would feel when I woke up in the morning. For example, I would wake up and feel uncomfortable and ugly in my skin. This would start off the cycle.

This would lead to the **craving** and fantasy of being thin and the feeling of starving. I would then obsess about how I could cut my calories even more than the day before. My **ritual** would include busying my diary around mealtimes so I wouldn't have time to eat. The **using** for me would be denying myself calories and restricting my food to give me a momentary boost. However, eventually I would eat something, such as a carrot stick, or I would not exercise the amount I thought I had to that day (which I could never do anyway because I was so weak from not feeding my body). As a result, I would feel **guilt** and shame. The next day I would feel the exact same as I did the previous morning. I kept going around and around, and no matter what I didn't eat or how much I exercised, it was never enough, because the level of what I wanted to achieve and what I wanted to look like kept changing. It started off by wanting to just lose a little bit of weight.

Of course, it wasn't actually about needing to lose weight, but more about how I felt inside. I didn't know this at the time. In fact, I didn't know this until years later. I didn't know that once I started on the journey of trying to change my body, it would then be a constant chase of the kilograms on the scale that would never be good enough.

This all makes me feel sad to write and acknowledge. Sad for that young woman who didn't realize what she was really searching for was peace of mind and contentment. Looking back, I can now see very clearly that this cycle kept repeating because I was trying to achieve the unachievable – filling the emptiness I felt with things and behaviours outside of myself. This lack of awareness, combined with the addiction, meant that my addictive behaviours were taking me away from myself as opposed to inward to a place of stability and self-worth.

Plastering Over a Hole

Now that we have delved into the repetitive cycles of addictive behaviour and seen that, when it comes to addiction, enough will never be enough, we need to ask ourselves: what hole are we trying to fill?

We need to focus on what our needs are, what triggers us to want to use and what we are trying to distract ourselves from. If we ignore what is causing the emotional trigger or ignore the hole within ourselves that we are trying to plaster over by using, we will find ourselves stuck in a cycle – wanting more to try to put a bigger and bigger bandage over a wound that isn't healing.

Finding out what the hole inside us is will only happen if we stop engaging in the cycle. That is why time without your drug or behaviour of choice is the only way recovery is possible, because we need to move through the discomfort and be with ourselves to realize that if we use anything external, it will not fix us or make us whole. Learning new ways to manage emotional triggers and negative feelings is one of the most important steps to stopping the repetitive cycle.

Now, some medications can be taken to help with cravings or withdrawal effects for some addictions, while others may be prescribed as a substitute (such as methadone for heroin addiction). Sometimes medications to help depression or anxiety might be offered, for example, if you use an addictive behaviour to self-medicate or improve your mood. Therefore, I would always recommend speaking to your doctor about any addiction you may have.

However, long-term addiction therapy focuses on understanding ourselves. Understanding the reasons why we use will stop us from falling back into relapse patterns. If our brains can learn our way into addiction, they can learn their way out again.[16]

ARE YOU EVER FULFILLED?

I want to close this chapter with some reflective questions. Take a moment to think about these carefully, and use your journal or a piece of paper to write down your thoughts.

Have you ever engaged in an addictive behaviour and thought to yourself, *okay, that's enough now, I'm satisfied,* then ended up coming back to it later down the line?

The next time you have the urge to engage in a behaviour or use a substance, ask yourself these questions:

- "Am I using this as a bandage for emotional wounds or as a distraction from the stress in my life?"
- "If I use a substance or engage in a behaviour, will it ever be enough to change what I am trying to heal or fix?"

In the previous chapter we talked about how a lot of addictive behaviours are commonplace in society, but they only become addictions when they negatively impact our lives. So, how do we determine what negative impact means? Well, what goes up, must come down, and our behaviours have consequences. But these consequences are sometimes necessary to prompt us to look at ourselves and our feelings in the first place. Let's take a closer look at those now.

CHAPTER 5
THE LOWS OF ADDICTION: WHAT GOES UP, MUST COME DOWN

Do We All Have to Hit Rock Bottom?

It seems only right that we talk about the lows of addiction after talking about the highs. Addiction can take people down some dark roads. I know this might sound depressing, but it's important to acknowledge that addiction can lead us into darkness – it's not all highs and adrenaline!

But I don't think suffering from addiction necessarily means that everyone will end up in the pits of despair. I think there is a spectrum of intensity with how people experience addictive behaviours, and I think our lows also vary from person to person. Therefore, I am going to explore the term "rock bottom" – not only what it means but also if we all must reach one before we decide to change.

Negative Consequences

We've seen that certain behaviours widely practiced in society – such as shopping, gaming, love or gambling –

only become problematic if we continue to engage in them despite experiencing negative consequences.

With drinking, many people in our culture drink alcohol, yet a lot of people have no problems attached to it. If anything, it may add value to what they're doing, whether it's a football game, dinner party or night out. People who do not suffer from addiction may run into problems, like drinking too much one night, but then they impose control. They can look at their drinking and become aware it's coming with a cost. They are then able to say to themselves, "I am going to drink less in the future", and they can stick to that.

Conversely, when an addict runs into problems, they tell themselves they will cut down and figure out how to be in control. Despite this, they are often unable to sustain these intentions.

So here we can see clearly that addiction is use accompanied by a cost of some sort. And this cost is driven by impaired control, meaning the addict can't reliably control their use. But when it comes to behavioural addictions, to gaming and social media, for example, where is the cost? In other words, what are the negative consequences?

Negative consequences sound quite vague, but that is because they can be very subjective. If you feel your addictive behaviour is impacting your life in some kind of harmful way, then it is worth reflecting on that.

The negative consequences of behavioural addiction can be more subtle than those of substance abuse, but they also affect the following areas of our lives:

- **Relationships:** Somebody with a social media addiction may alienate their partner by staying glued to their phone, or someone with workaholism may miss their child's first steps because they were at the office.
- **Finances:** Someone with a gaming addiction may spend more than they had planned on loot boxes or subscriptions to premium game services, or someone with a love

addiction may overextend their budget paying for dates or gifts for their partner.

- **Work:** Someone with a social media addiction may be so distracted by their profiles that their performance on the job diminishes.
- **Health:** Somebody with a gaming addiction may experience wrist or thumb pain, or somebody struggling with bulimia may have dental issues from excessive purging after eating.

WHAT IS THE COST OF YOUR ADDICTIVE BEHAVIOUR?

Now I want you to write down any negative consequences you may experience relating to your substance use or addictive behaviour in your journal. Although the above categories are not exhaustive, keep them in mind while you do this exercise and try to think of additional areas of your life that may be affected.

Rock Bottom

You may have heard the term "hit rock bottom". Just like the phrase "rock-bottom prices" is used in advertising to suggest that prices can't go any lower, if a person hits rock bottom, then they are at their lowest ebb. A crisis point. Peers I've spoken to in recovery have described this as the moment they could finally see the damage they were doing to themselves, and that change was needed. But does everyone need to go through this?

There is no absolutely definitive evidence to suggest that reaching rock bottom will cause change, or that everybody has one. But there has been research on the subject, not to mention numerous stories of trauma bringing people lasting, positive change.

The psychologist Abraham Maslow suggested that there might be a connection between someone experiencing turmoil then undergoing personal development. He felt that traumas – or "nadir experiences" – can be important learning events that can initiate a transformation to a person's outlook and character.[1 2]

Richard Tedeschi and Lawrence Calhoun defined this as "post-traumatic growth"[3] and suggested it could lead to developing more fulfilling relationships, increased confidence, an improved sense of purpose or a greater appreciation of life.[4]

In 1988, the cruise ship *Jupiter* tragically sank near the Greek port of Piraeus, killing four people. Some of the survivors were surveyed by Stephen Joseph,[5] and of those, 94 per cent felt that they "[did] not take life for granted anymore", and 91 per cent "[valued] their relationships much more now".[6 7]

This clearly traumatic event caused some to have a more positive outlook on life, and their lives improved as a result. But what has this got to do with addiction? Well, we may experience a traumatic experience because of it – such as an overdose or car accident. This can be a powerful wake-up call that initiates the kind of personal transformation we need. But surely not everyone who recovers from addiction needs to suffer an overdose or life-threatening injury?

Dramatic transformations have also been found to occur following a period of psychological turmoil, including addiction.[8 9 10] In other words, addiction is a trauma in itself. It can lead people down a painful never-ending path of loss and suffering. People suffering from addiction may not see any hope of breaking free from the addictive cycle; they may not understand that a different way of living is possible. When this happens, they may sink deeper and deeper, leading to an accidental overdose, while some unfortunately see no other choice but to take their own life. I must add if you feel you are in danger of self-harm, please speak to a doctor or call an ambulance.

But how exactly does an addict begin the journey up from rock bottom? One theory from Dr Russell Stagg is that a nadir experience, including addiction, is the very lowest point of life, where we suffer "the loss of a predictable and safe world".[11] This leaves us feeling powerless and empty, what Stagg calls the threshold phase. Following this, we realize we need to make changes: we may need to change our identity, the company we keep and what we want out of life. Steven Foster and Meredith Little described this process as a "threshing place", where the part of the grain that is not important falls away.[12]

The above research indicates that traumatic experiences can apparently cause lasting change for the better, but the question remains: does everyone have to hit rock bottom before they recover?

The problem that arises with thinking that we all have a rock bottom is that we then might wait until we reach it before we change. This could be an excuse to continue engaging in our behaviour or using our substance. Saying "It could be worse", or "I'll know when I need to stop" only keeps us engaged in the self-destructive cycle.

I spoke to Francis Lickerish, addiction specialist, and asked about his experience with clients. He said he didn't think there is such a thing as a literal rock bottom, because things can always get worse.[13] In his experience, he has encountered some people who recognize they've got a problem and immediately deal with it before it has any serious negative impact, and other people who, due to their addiction, have sadly died. So it seems there doesn't necessarily have to be a trauma or struggle – some people can realize that their behaviours are getting in the way of what they want to get out of life, and this leads them to do something about it.

Therefore, I would suggest that rock bottom is actually just the moment we decide we want to make a change. This can be a light-bulb moment, either because we are tired of feeling sick and tired or because we've come to realize the impact of our addictive behaviours. This is highly personal and varies from addiction to addiction. The reality is that everyone's lowest point is subjective and can cause its own impact or its own kind of suffering, regret or self-loathing.

As I mentioned earlier, with behavioural addictions it's often harder to see how these addictive behaviours are negatively affecting our lives. One of my clients with a gaming addiction couldn't identify any serious consequences of it at first – he was still able to go out and live his life, socialize, exercise and eat a balanced diet. However, that year he had set himself some goals that he wanted to achieve and realized, while he was playing a game, that he hadn't achieved any of them. This became his rock bottom as he felt it was becoming too much a part of his life.

Rock bottom can also manifest as a family or friend intervention. We can be in total denial around our behaviours until we are met with an ultimatum from those closest to us. Sometimes it might take the realization that our behaviours are hurting those we love to make us see that we need to change.

Honesty is the Best Policy (Especially With Ourselves!)

I think it's safe to say that, since there are so many factors affecting people's choice to change, there is no one-size-fits-all approach to recovery. But self-reflection is certainly an integral tool to acknowledging when you need to make a change. It's important to be honest when we ask ourselves: are we looking to soothe how we feel internally by engaging in these addictive behaviours without focusing on the source of the problem?

Looking closely at these behaviours under a microscope can help you reflect on their purpose. By understanding their perceived benefits, you can recognize what needs the behaviours are fulfilling. By understanding the lows, you can identify the cost these behaviours may bring. This can prompt us to make a change, for example, pursuing alternatives that are more creative or fulfilling such as singing, dancing, drawing, colouring or drama.

Being Powerless

What really helped me peek through my denial was when I came across the first step of AA: "admitting we are powerless". It means that no amount of trying or self-control will change the way alcohol or drugs affect our brain. It is as if we are allergic to it. With addictive behaviours, think of it more that we are powerless over the effect the behaviour has on us. This really helped me understand that I am not in control, and I don't get to choose how substances or behaviours affect me. I can only choose to engage with them or not.

So, if you are not sure whether you've hit rock bottom, ask yourself these two questions: are you powerless over your behaviour or substance? And is it stopping you from achieving your goals?

Admitting powerlessness can often be seen as a weakness by those who are in the early stages of recovery, but in fact, admitting we are powerless is a sign of strength and letting go. It's a sign we are surrendering to things out of our control, which means we need to learn to trust a wider community, including friends, family or even our therapist. Some of us might have been conditioned to believe we have to fix all our problems on our own. Therefore, learning a different way of dealing with things can feel very uncomfortable.

Powerless does not mean helpless, and this is a very important distinction. You are never powerless over your actions, your decisions or your relationships. When you admit to powerlessness, you are admitting to being powerless over your drinking, drug use, gambling or any other addictive behaviour. Therefore, saying we are powerless is not an excuse to keep going down the same destructive path; it's about surrender. It means we must stop fighting and instead be open to change.

I really struggled with this concept of powerlessness at the beginning of my recovery. Of course I believed I had control over how much I drank. Or that I was in control over when I was going to stop losing weight. But I was very wrong. Letting go and admitting that I couldn't do it on my own were big steps toward freedom.

When I was in treatment at Start2Stop, an addiction centre, one of the first groups that I was introduced to was a "Powerless and Damages" group. The groups aimed to explore the destructive moments of our using. The purpose of this group wasn't to shame us, but to revisit certain times in our using that we had been powerless over our addiction and show the damages we had caused as a result of our using. This didn't just have to be the damage we caused others, but the damage we caused ourselves or the danger we put ourselves in.

I would always dread this group as the shame became tangible and I found it overwhelmingly confronting. I would also compare my damages to everyone else's as a way of telling myself I didn't need to be there.

However, the power of group therapy meant that I never felt judged as others were also sharing their feelings of shame. It helped remind me that my behaviours were not healthy and that I had been self-destructive for some time. This encouraged me to acknowledge my powerlessness, which consequently helped me move forward toward a newer, brighter life.

DAMAGES AND CONSEQUENCES

So, I want to give you an opportunity to dig a bit deeper into your possible powerlessness and the consequences of your behaviours. This is not to shame you but to highlight your possible self-destructive patterns and to acknowledge that you might not really be in control.

I want you to think about a time that you felt you couldn't stop the behaviour you were engaging in, whether that was using a substance or engaging in a behaviour. This could be a time when you hadn't planned on using or engaging in a behaviour but found yourself doing it anyway. Write out the scenario in as much detail as possible. Can you remember what happened before you started? Had you promised yourself you'd only have one or two drinks but then ended up having many more? Did you put a time limit on your social media use but ended up losing track of time or even turning off the alarm reminder?

Once you describe the scenario, I want you to write out any of the consequences or damages that ensued in bullet-point formation in your journal or on a piece of paper. This might be confronting, but will help you objectively identify the negative impact of your behaviours.

The Final Straw

Some people's situations will mean that their rock bottom is more traumatic than others, but ultimately the final straw is when you decide you've had enough. Perhaps even reading this book shows that you yourself have decided to make a change.

Just remember, we don't all have to hit a dramatic rock bottom in order to change. A lot of the time it's more about facing how our addiction affects our life and asking ourselves if we want that for our future. I am by no means saying this is easy, but I think it's important to know that we do have a choice. Once we have acknowledged that, then we need to take responsibility for it (this can be the hard part!).

Without a doubt, addiction is a set of problems, but recovery is also a set of problems. Recovery is painful, uncomfortable, sometimes lonely and can feel alienating. But so is addiction. The difference is that addiction gets more and more painful whereas recovery gets less and less painful over time.

Recovery is all about the process, and I'm always saying this to my clients. The most important thing to remember in early recovery is that this process takes time. Nothing changes overnight, and there will be barriers to overcome along the way.

So now I want to look a little more closely at one of these major barriers, something that might be stopping us from even acknowledging we are experiencing rock bottom: denial.

CHAPTER 6
CAN WE HANDLE THE TRUTH?

Are We Stuck in Denial?

I am aware the last chapter was pretty heavy, and I promise you that there is light at the end of the tunnel. But, if the lows are so horrible, and they increase the level of shame that we experience, why do we continue to repeat our behaviours?

Looking at it from the outside, you may know friends who are going through these lows but for some unfathomable reason can't see they have a problem, let alone want to change. You yourself may be having a similar experience. Therefore, I want to talk to you about what keeps us stuck in these lows: denial. Denial is such a powerful defence mechanism that it can keep us in very self-destructive cycles.

COST–BENEFIT ANALYSIS

In previous exercises, I asked you to write down the highs of the addictive behaviours that you engage in and also the lows. Is the list of lows longer than the highs? If so, write down the reasons that you might still continue to engage in these behaviours.

So, how do we spot denial? How do we help someone who is in denial? Let's look a little closer at why we find it hard to handle the truth.

What Is Denial?

We have finally reached the part of the book where we mention Freud. Sigmund Freud (1856–1939) was a famous psychologist whose theories formed the foundations of modern psychology.

Freud developed the idea of "ego defences" or defence mechanisms that we unconsciously use to protect us from negative feelings such as anxiety or guilt. These negative feelings occur when we have upsetting thoughts or we feel threatened. Freud felt that these defence mechanisms make us distort our reality to allow us to cope with a situation.

We all use defence mechanisms in our everyday life. They act to filter all the thoughts that go through our heads each day and stop us from worrying about everything at once. We wouldn't be able to function very efficiently without them.[1]

However, sometimes these defence mechanisms can go into overdrive.

Lots of different types of defence mechanisms have been theorized over the years. Here are some examples:

- **Projection:** This occurs when we attribute our negative feelings, such as shame, onto someone else. Projection allows us to acknowledge the presence of the feeling but not fully recognize it within ourselves. For example, if we feel shame about cheating on our partner, we may become jealous and accuse them of infidelity.
- **Rationalization:** This happens when we may think of an explanation to justify our actions. For example, we may justify stealing from somebody because we tell ourselves that we needed the money more than them.

- **Intellectualization:** This occurs when we overanalyse a situation in order to distance ourselves from our emotions. For example, if we are diagnosed with an illness, instead of facing our feelings about our mortality, we research everything we can about the condition.
- **Minimization:** This happens when we diminish our problems by dismissing their impact or consequences. For example, saying, "I might skip lectures to play games, no one learns anything from them anyway."
- **Compensation:** This occurs when we focus on achieving in one part of our lives to compensate for insecurities in another part. For example, we may dedicate all our time and effort to our occupation to avoid difficulties in our home life.[2] [3] [4]

It was actually Freud's daughter Anna who added denial to the list of recognized defence mechanisms.

We are probably all familiar with the concept of being in denial. It's commonly used to describe someone who can't see something that is obvious to everyone else. It occurs when someone ignores uncomfortable thoughts, events or facts, either by blocking them out of their mind or refusing to acknowledge them as fact. These realities could include an illness, a financial difficulty, a partner's infidelity or, of course, an addiction.[5] If we do not believe that something bad has happened or is happening, then we think it cannot hurt us. It is an emotional rejection of the truth.[6] [7]

I guess you could say that denial keeps us safe. It is a way we can temporarily avoid intense emotion. If you are experiencing something traumatic, perhaps the loss of something or someone in your life, denial creates this slight distance between us and the emotion.

For example, Dr Kübler-Ross proposed the five stages of grief after observing her terminally ill patients and their families. The first stage is denial, which is sometimes accompanied by shock, followed by anger, bargaining, depression and then acceptance.[8] Kübler-Ross saw that denial typically occurred straight after the bereavement. It seemed that denial, like Anna Freud suggested, was protecting the bereaved from the pain and allowed some time for them to adjust to this new reality.[9]

Denial may be a natural part of the grieving process, but it becomes problematic when used as a shield to keep us from recognizing when our addictive behaviours are becoming destructive. The same goes for the other types of defence mechanisms I listed on pages 86–87. All of these can lead us to continue to act in a way that negatively impacts our lives and our health. As these defence mechanisms' function is to protect us from emotional discomfort, it can be difficult to avoid using them. But recovery is almost impossible if a person does not believe they are in an addictive cycle in the first place.

Going forward, I will use the term "denial" as an umbrella term for these defence mechanisms for the sake of simplicity.

What Does Denial in Addiction Look Like?

During the first session, new clients often do not want me to look at their addictive behaviour or substance use. Instead, they want me to help them figure out why bad things keep happening to them. Essentially, they want to change for the better but don't want to change their behaviours. They are stuck in a cycle of experiencing bad things but are not able to see that the common denominator is, in fact, themselves. Some tell me that their partner has given them an ultimatum because they no longer want to put up with their substance use or addictive behaviour. Even in this instance, when one of the closest people to them is telling them they can see a problem, the client is adamant that their partner is overreacting.

So what might denial look like in addictive behaviours?

- **Compensation:** Achieving a high level or rank in a game to distract yourself from social anxiety in "real life". For example, "I can't to go to the party because I have to practice for my upcoming online tournament".
- **Minimization:** This could come in the form of downplaying our behaviour and suggesting that an addict would partake in this behaviour constantly. For example, "I only shop when I am at home". Alternatively, it could be suggesting that it could be worse, or defining extreme circumstances as where the bar is for our behaviour to be a problem. For example, "I drank last night, but I didn't black out".
- **Blaming others:** Justifying our behaviour as a consequence of an external factor or another person's actions. For example, "I am on my phone all the time because you are always watching that stupid programme".
- **Projection:** Placing our own negative feelings about our addiction onto someone else's behaviour. For example, if somebody who feels guilty for their drinking gossips to someone else, "I was shocked about how much 'x' drank last night, she really made a fool of herself".
- **Rationalization:** Giving excuses to make our behaviour acceptable. For example, "Gambling online relaxes me so I'm nice to be around".
- **Beliefs of control:** We might tell ourselves that we can stop when we want to even if there is a lot of evidence to the contrary. For example, "I can have just one drink".

REFLECTING ON YOUR JUSTIFICATIONS

Take a look at the last exercise (Cost–Benefit Analysis on page 85) and your reasons to keep engaging in your behaviour. Do any of them look like any of the examples above? On your list, highlight the ones that fit with the above examples so that they stand out.

For some people, being supportively challenged by the facts might be enough to bring about change. However, some people may have developed such strong defences to avoid these unacceptable feelings that they will remain in denial despite stark evidence of a possible addiction.

Why Are We in Denial?

We've looked at denial as a defence mechanism protecting us from uncomfortable thoughts or experiences. But what kind of uncomfortable thoughts and experiences are we talking about?

At face value, somebody with an addictive behaviour may subconsciously use denial to protect them from the idea that they are addicted and any shame they may feel around that. For example, they may consider it a weakness or feel that they have let their family down.

Denial can also protect people from coming to terms with the consequences of their addiction. These could be health effects such as liver disease, financial problems from gambling or damaged relationships because of love addiction. This denial allows them to continue to use and continue to experience the perceived benefits or highs of their addiction without acknowledging the consequences. If we realize the highs come with lows, then we won't be able to cling to the highs anymore.

Crucially, denial also serves the purpose of protecting the user from any uncomfortable truths that may have caused their addiction in the first place. For example, if someone realizes that they gain their sense of self-worth from work, they may have to come to terms with the fact that they were not invited to take over the family business and therefore never felt good enough.

But also, as addicts, if we are in denial, we don't have to take responsibility for our actions. We also don't have to acknowledge the fact that we are not totally in control of our lives and what happens to us in the future. The same goes for being kept in a safe, familiar cycle. If we are in denial, we will be stuck in a repetitive cycle that inevitably keeps us from having to change. How do I know this? Because I was exactly the same.

In *The Psychology of Addiction*, Jenny Svanberg argues that to change is to challenge our essence. Those who are engaging in addictive behaviours perceive any challenges around their behaviours as an attack on who they are or want to be. Therefore, of course, they will want to hide behind denial.[10]

For example, I had a client who took part in ultramarathons as well as triathlons. It was becoming destructive, and her health was deteriorating as a result. Her family were very active and had encouraged her to exercise her whole life, otherwise she might be considered lazy. Therefore, the idea that her exercise could be damaging and addictive was something she found very hard to grasp. She was also worried she would lose the respect and approval of her parents if she stopped taking part in these races. Exercise was a way she communicated with others, and it was her whole identity. The denial she was experiencing was an attempt to protect herself from such a massive challenge to her identity.

There are other reasons that someone might be in denial. People close to the addicted person may be encouraging or enabling their destructive behaviour.[11] There is also some evidence that those addicted to certain substances may have impaired thought processes, which may mean they lack insight into their use.[12]

From the outside, someone's denial can be a source of frustration, sadness or anger to those around them. However, if we try to understand where this denial comes from, we can be more compassionate and patient about it. There is an argument that denial should not be called denial at all. This is because the term places a stigma on those with addiction. The term fails to illustrate the role of denial in protecting us from the shame, trauma or distress that make us turn to addictive behaviours in the first place.

Denial and Relationships

Above I mentioned that someone close to an addicted person may encourage their destructive behaviour. You might be wondering why anybody would facilitate someone else's addiction. Well, it is because people do not like change.

Therapist Francis Lickerish explained to me that denial can run deep in some families. He views intensity and drama as an avoidance technique.[13] If someone in the family is addicted and creates drama, then the other members of the family can concentrate on that rather than looking at their own problems. This may mean that the family will subconsciously work to keep the addiction going. For example, a married couple may not love each other anymore, and the relationship has broken down. As a result, their child has picked up on this disharmony at home, has become unhappy or angry and has started using drugs. The parents may, without knowing, focus on their child's drug use and put all their energy into putting out the fires that their child's drug use creates. This could act as a distraction from their marital problems.

Addiction can sometimes be the glue that keeps a marriage together. If the glue is taken away, then the marriage falls apart. Unfortunately, some marriages do not survive recovery.

Dealing With Denial

I spoke to some family members of addicts who explained to me what it is like to see their loved one in denial. The key indicator in terms of recognizing denial was that whenever they tried to talk to them about how they were doing, they would be met with an abrupt answer. For example, "I don't want to talk about it" or "There is nothing wrong".

This can be very hard as the family member can clearly see that the addicted person is in distress and their life is becoming unmanageable. The sad reality is that if an addict is in denial, there is not much anyone can do to make them think otherwise. This can be very difficult to accept; it can make us feel powerless. There are support groups for this if you find yourself in this situation, and I will touch on that later.

Confrontation

Denial can make an addict resist requests from their friends and family to change, especially if they are directly challenged. They might become argumentative or irritated by any questioning. So, should we directly confront people about their denial if it is going to get their back up? Well, there is strong evidence to suggest that direct, forceful or antagonistic approaches are not very effective in persuading someone to change their perceptions or break through their denial. In fact, labelling someone as being stuck in deep denial and not motivated to change is seen as quite unhelpful. The denial is there to protect us, so when we feel attacked our defences increase and we are less likely to change.[14] [15]

Supporting Someone in Denial

Instead, I would recommend an empathetic, compassionate and supportive approach. Sometimes that can be difficult, but there is evidence to suggest that this method brings a more desirable outcome. For example, one study found that a family's gentler, sympathetic approach was twice as successful in persuading an addict to go to treatment compared to a confrontational one.[16]

As we have seen, the reasons why somebody becomes addicted are complex. Often they are using or behaving in a way to help them cope with difficult experiences. Al-Anon – a support group for relatives of alcoholics – defines alcoholism as a family disease.[17] Often the family dynamic, through nature or nurture, plays a key role in initiating addictive behaviour. Therefore, to confront someone or be angry at them will likely just exacerbate the reasons they are using in the first place. Instead of shaming someone, we should try to understand. As Gabor Maté eloquently puts it, "It is not what we do that has the greatest impact, but who we are being as we do it. Loving parent or prosecutor? Friend or judge?"[18] Often a confrontational method will instigate further shame, embarrassment and a breakdown in our relationship with the addicted person.

That isn't to say that it isn't important to challenge, set boundaries and provide constructive feedback. One technique I recommend to my clients when they want to approach someone in denial is "coming from a place of I". This allows us to express how someone's actions make us feel without sounding persecutory or judgemental. For example:

- "I feel sad and detached from you when you are on your phone at dinner."
- "I feel scared when you take drugs and then shout at me."
- "When you have to stay late at work, I miss you and I want to spend more quality time together."
- "When you spend all your income on betting, I worry about our financial situation."

It is easier said than done, but one thing I recommend is staying calm. Remember, the price of denial's protection is the inability to seek help.[19] Sometimes the person in denial will get defensive or irritated. If you respond in anger, it may escalate the situation and increase their resistance. By being kind and gentle, even if they don't react the way you want them to, you may plant the first seeds in their mind that change is needed.

Boundaries can be the most important thing to a family member or friend in keeping them safe. They can also prevent someone from becoming codependent with the addict. We should not try to enable the addicted person. The hardest part to acknowledge is that, as a friend or family member, you are unable to make an addict change their behaviours. That can be tough.

Another thing you can do is therapy. You can do this just for yourself, or you can encourage the addict to try it with you. To create your own safe space where you find support can be very beneficial in helping you keep boundaries in place.

Therapy works collaboratively with a person in treatment to overcome their denial. It tries to chip away at the denial over time by highlighting the person's addictive behaviours and the consequences of the addiction. This encourages the person with the addiction to face their uncomfortable reality rather than block it out. If the person is unable or unwilling to go to treatment or engage with therapy, then this approach could be something you could try with them.

Feeling Challenged?

Defence mechanisms are something we all have. In some way, shape or form, we all have thoughts or feelings that protect us from some harsh truths. They might help us persevere when the odds are against us, but they may also act as a barrier to active, positive change.

I encourage you to think about how you felt when someone challenged your addictive behaviour. Has anyone ever mentioned something about how much time or money you spend on something? What did you think when they pointed this out? Did you get frustrated or defensive? Perhaps this book will help you make your first steps in challenging your perceptions about your substance use or addictive behaviour.

Sometimes it can be helpful to look at objective evidence. Do you have "screen time" on your phone that can tell you how often you are looking at it? Can you use an app to log how much alcohol you drink per week?

If you have a friend or family member who is going through addiction, try to understand why this person is engaging in addictive behaviour, bearing in mind it's not your responsibility to fix them. It is important to acknowledge their actions, especially if they are harming you in some way, but if you do find yourself confronting them with aggression or frustration, try to consider your influence with that person and ask yourself if challenging them in this way is helpful. If you can help them identify the reason for their addictive behaviour and help them realize the effect their behaviour has on their life, then it could help them question their reality in a way that encourages positive change.

A bit like therapy, I want this book to gently chip away at your denial and spark something within you to take a second look. This might be the start of something great.

CHAPTER 7
BREAKING THE PATTERNS

How Do We Change Our Habitual Patterns and Behaviours?

Why do we find change difficult? If we want to stop doing something, why can't we just stop doing it? Aside from the challenges of physical addiction, what stops us from changing?

In life, change is inevitable: we move home, change career and see friends come and go. Though often it feels more comfortable to hold on to existing patterns, this might not make us happy and lead us to a life we want. This chapter is all about change and how breaking harmful patterns of behaviour can be rewarding and necessary if we want to live free from an addictive cycle.

Before we dive in, I want to say that a lot of us fear change. As humans, we are programmed to find comfort in our routines, and we often surround ourselves with people who have habits similar to ours. Often our habits are based in deep-rooted beliefs about ourselves and therefore can be difficult to break.

In my experience, my whole identity once revolved around being the party girl and all the drinking and drug-taking that came with it. Making a change meant questioning who I was. That was scary, but I promise you it's not impossible. We will have a look at the different stages of change and how we can break bad habits and form new, healthy ones!

Belief Systems

As I have spoken about earlier in the book, belief systems are the filters that we see our world through. These include deeply embedded beliefs about ourselves that have been with us since childhood.

You may have heard of cognitive behavioural therapy (CBT), which was first developed by Aaron Beck in the 1960s and 1970s. He based this on the "cognitive model", which proposed that dysfunctional thinking is common in all psychological conditions. Generally speaking, the cognitive model suggests there are three levels of cognitions, either healthy or unhealthy. These are:

1. **Core beliefs or belief systems:** Our strongly held beliefs about ourselves and the world around us. These are often inflexible and can form the basis of how we perceive our day-to-day experiences. For example, "I am unlovable" or "I am not worthy of…"
2. **Underlying assumptions:** These are intermediate beliefs and tend to be more specific than the core beliefs. Described by Melanie Fennell as "rules for living", these are what we think we need to do to compensate for these negative beliefs.[1] For example, "I will be rejected if I do not please people."
3. **Automatic thoughts:** These happen at the most superficial level and are spontaneous reactions to something that has happened. For example, if we have to say no to someone, we might think, "I haven't pleased them so they are now going to hate me."[2 3 4]

Let's say that you see someone you know across the street, and they do not wave at you. One way of viewing the situation is "That person didn't see me". However, if you have a negative core belief, such as "I am not likeable", then you may view the situation differently and think "That person didn't acknowledge me as she wanted to avoid me". This thought ("she avoided me") can also provide a feedback loop that further feeds into that core belief ("I am unlikeable").[5]

Belief systems are often developed during our experiences in childhood and adolescence. These experiences can include parental divorce, bereavement, bullying, physical or sexual abuse, living in poverty or being the subject of discrimination. These formative experiences can also be more subtle, such as receiving less attention than a sibling.[6]

Belief systems can influence how we act in certain situations. As we have discussed previously, we might engage in self-destructive behaviours as a by-product of our belief system. For example, our belief that we are unlovable unless we please others could cause us to do something that doesn't feel comfortable just to fit in.

One of my deeply embedded belief systems is "I am too much". A close family member used to call me a SPULG (spoilt pushy unpleasant little girl) in moments that I can only remember being myself – loud and carefree. As a result, for a lot of my life I have felt that I am too much for other people and therefore I am unlovable.

CHALLENGING OUR SELF-BELIEFS

Now I want you to try an exercise that will challenge some of your self-beliefs.

Take some time to think about something negative that you have thought about yourself. Perhaps it's a belief that started when you were a child, one that was formed by what someone said to you or what you experienced.

Maybe this belief follows you around all the time without you even realizing it. It could be a belief that you may be in denial about. Do you ever believe you are not enough? Do you ever believe you are too much? Do you ever believe you are a failure? Do you ever believe you are not worthy of being in a happy, loving relationship?

Let's look at what you believe about yourself in the context of your addiction. Do you ever believe that you can't be happy or fun without alcohol or mood-altering substances? Do you ever believe that if you choose a path of recovery you will have failed?

Now take each belief you have and try to reframe it by asking yourself: What proof do I have that the belief is a reality? Is this belief keeping me stuck in a cycle of denial?

Habits

Of course, we talked about the addictive cycle and habit formation previously. I think by now we are probably neuroscienced out, so I will keep it very simple here. Habits are largely automatic actions that we often do subconsciously. In fact, experiments on rats showed that the habit parts of their brains automatically started and stopped a habitual behaviour even though the rats might have been doing something else. This means that when I want to brush my teeth, I can easily do this in the background while looking at my phone or walking around the house.[7] [8] Therefore, we can engage in habits almost without realizing it. This makes them difficult to break!

As I mentioned earlier, habits can also be positively reinforced if we are rewarded by doing them (remember that dopamine hit?) and can be triggered by cues that are associated with their formation. For example, going to the bar might trigger that almost automatic habit of going outside for a cigarette and receiving the "reward" of nicotine.

Some habits are also thought to reflect our belief systems, goals and values. So, if our belief systems are negative, then our habits are not going to be loving or contribute to a healthy lifestyle. To use a simple example, in the past there was an association between smoking and being cool. Some adolescents therefore sought to achieve social acceptance by smoking. This created a feedback loop where habits and behaviours ("To fit in, I need to smoke") fed more and more into negative belief systems ("I am unlikeable and so need to please others").

If our habits are interlinked with the way we think about ourselves, then forming new habits while working on our belief systems can help us reforge these feedback loops and create healthier ones. I tell my clients that the outsides of their life have to change if they want the insides to change.

UNCONSCIOUS HABITS

Let's see if your habits reflect your belief systems. Can you think about one of your habits? Something you do perhaps automatically and unconsciously? I want you to write down any emotions you have when you do them. These can be positive or negative. How do they make you feel about yourself? Do you feel guilt or do you beat yourself up?

So, now that we know what belief systems are, and how habits are formed, how do we go about changing them?

Difficulty With Change

Albert Einstein said that the definition of insanity was when we repeat the same thing over and over but expect different results. This is a very good way to describe what happens when we are in an addictive cycle – we always hope that things won't end in the same way that they have been for months or even years.

Now, I don't necessarily believe that doing the same thing over again and expecting different results is "insanity", but it is a common trap that most of us fall into during our lives. So, to encompass change in our lives and create different results, we need to act differently than before.

Some of our habits have been with us since childhood. We have already discussed how substances and behaviours like gambling can alter our brain function, give us cravings or make us withdraw. But what about change in general – what other factors can get in the way of us making real change?

The Fear of Change

There is evidence that we humans, and in fact all animals, have an innate urge to feel in control.[9] After all, there wouldn't be any incentive to face up to challenges if we didn't feel we had the ability to control our circumstances and overcome the accompanying obstacles. Our routines give us a feeling of familiarity, of comfort and safety.[10] Therefore, it stands to reason that we do not like uncertainty and tend to have a fear of the unknown. An old therapist of mine used to call change the "C word", as change is something so many of us dread.

You've probably heard the expression "The devil you know is better than the devil you don't". I think that sums up our human psyche pretty well and explains why we may stay in a situation that isn't necessarily healthy for us.

The Fear of Change in Identity

The deep-rooted belief system that forms the basis of how we think or react to certain situations is often what we build our own personal identity around. For example, if I feel I am not good enough, and that to compensate I have to work harder than everyone else, I might identify myself as a "hard worker". I would feel rewarded by working hard, I may feel guilty if I take a sick day and I may feel particularly offended if someone questions my work ethic. This identity gives us something to rely on; it gives us a sense of control over our lives and our current surroundings. This often lifelong identity can be difficult to change, and to admit that our belief system is actually self-destructive might be difficult to come to terms with. Challenging our identity may require a re-evaluation of the company we keep, the goals we have set and the coping mechanisms we have nurtured throughout our lives.[11] Remember when we talked about ego defences? Denial can protect us from these hard-hitting questions.

The Loss That Comes With Change

With every change we experience comes a loss, and with every loss comes grief. There is no right or wrong way to experience grief, and when it comes to breaking patterns, everyone will experience this differently.

The losses we experience with change aren't always tangible, and I am not just talking about the loss of the specific behaviour itself. For example, if you are deciding to go sober, there will be a loss of not just the alcohol but perhaps all the upcoming events you have in your life: the parties, events and birthdays that you had planned around the alcohol. There is a loss around who you were when you were drinking. The loss of the "mask" perhaps that you were able to access when using alcohol.

Another example I have experienced personally is the loss of the body that an eating disorder gives you. Who are you without the tiny frame you've been forcing your body to be? And what happens if you lose people's attention or concerns about your health? These were questions I had to face if I was to move forward with my recovery.

Change and Relationships

Changing patterns of behaviours and habits can also be interlinked with our relationships. If we look at our addictive behaviours, we might see that we tend to normalize our substance use or behaviours by surrounding ourselves with people who use similarly. Whether it's drinking habits, gaming habits or shopping habits, if we surround ourselves with people who are engaging in the same habits as us, it will be harder for us to change.

For example, there are many people who say that after a long day at work, they need a glass of wine to relax. If you're friends with people who do this, it will of course encourage you to do the same. It justifies your behaviour and means you never question the glass of wine that you have at the end of the day.

These days, the same can be said for the use of social media. If the people you surround yourself with are into posting a lot of content or spending a lot of time creating content to post online, this will more likely be a focus of yours too.

I see this pattern of behaviour a lot with clients who are students. These clients come to me regarding their relationship to alcohol, and they can't understand why, even though they drink the same amount as everyone else, they seem to be having more serious consequences or higher levels of anxiety. Their friends tell them that they don't have a problem with alcohol as they are drinking the same amount as everyone else, but what my clients aren't taking into consideration is that most of their friends are using problematically.

The difficulty we face when we want to change our patterns of behaviour is that we can't change other people's behaviours. We can only change our own. We also can't guarantee that we will have the support of others when changing a behaviour, especially if we have been engaging in it with these same people.

A real challenge for me was that my drinking was linked to other people's behaviours and habits, and I sought comfort in that for a very long time. My friends found it surprising that I had made the decision to stop drinking, and I was met with some judgement and lots of questioning. I found it very difficult to break out of the patterns inherent in certain friendships as in the past I had gotten a lot of validation and approval from our shared drinking habits. But in hindsight, most of these friendships didn't run that deep anyway since they centred around going out and the drama that surrounded that.

How Can We Bring About Change?

Change can be difficult. But don't worry, we are going to talk about how we can break these patterns of behaviours. The cognitive model that we talked about at the beginning of this chapter (see page 98) suggests that to bring about change we should address all of these levels of thought. Modifying the automatic thoughts down to the core beliefs can bring lasting change. This means breaking our old habits, removing ourselves from certain situations and people that reinforce those habits, replacing the old habits with new habits and potentially starting therapy.

Abstinence

When it comes to addiction or addictive behaviours, the first change needs to be abstinence. Abstinence from substances is refraining from using. However, abstinence from behavioural addictions can be more nuanced.

In our chapter on the lows of addiction, we talked about withdrawal, our reduced ability to gain pleasure from stimuli other than the addictive substance, and the hormonal imbalance in our brains. In *Dopamine Nation*, Dr Anna Lembke recommends roughly 30 days of abstinence to help rebalance the chemicals – like dopamine – in our brains.[12] This duration of abstinence also helps to create enough space between us and the substance in question. Of course, this can vary depending on the person and the addiction.

I would like to stress that a period of abstinence from some substances, such as alcohol, benzodiazepines and opioids, can be life-threatening without medical help and monitoring. For a substance addiction, I recommend speaking to a medical professional before considering a period of abstinence.

When we think of abstinence, it is important that we try not to think of it as abstaining forever. It feels like too big of a mountain to climb in one go, especially as we're not used to abstaining from our behaviour or drug. If we think of abstaining forever, that might only create fear of "never feeling happy" or "never being excited about things again".

While this might feel like a reality, we are not helping ourselves by projecting into the future. The programme of AA suggests that we must abstain or stay sober "Just for today". If we can get our head onto our pillow at the end of the day without using our behaviour or substance, this is a huge win. This helps us recognize our achievement at the end of each day while slowly starting to learn that we don't "need" to use.

While working with clients who have been trying to abstain from different addictive behaviours, I have heard them use the narrative "I'm too weak and that's why I can't stop". In the moments we are craving it feels like we do not have a choice, but we always do. However, if we give in, we won't have a choice about how much we will use or when we will stop.

Let's take my client G for example. He struggles to understand why once he has had just one sip of alcohol, he can't guarantee A) when he will have his final drink that evening, B) whether or not he will black out and C) how he will behave. What he does know for certain is that if he makes the very difficult choice not to drink on a night out, he will A) not black out, B) end up at home when he decides and C) know how he will behave. It all comes down to the first drink, because as soon as he has a sip, the addiction is "activated", and he is out of control.

Abstaining From Behavioural Addictions

With behavioural disorders such as smartphone addiction, eating disorders or sex addiction, abstinence is not as simple as just giving up the destructive behaviour. Unlike abstinence from alcohol, where we can stop drinking altogether, we cannot simply give up certain necessary behaviours.

With eating disorders, abstinence is more commonly seen as sticking to a structured meal plan. Eating three meals and two to three snacks a day every day and not manipulating this plan is practicing abstinence. Having a weekly meal plan that you discuss with either a nutritionist or someone who has a healthy relationship to food can help you feel more able to let go of the control around food.

When it comes to behavioural addictions in relationships, the fact is that we are social creatures, and living in isolation is likely to be inappropriate. Instead, we must ask ourselves how we can abstain from certain behaviours to encourage healthier relationships. Perhaps that looks like putting in more boundaries with people or setting yourself some rules about how often you sleep with a new partner. These boundaries can be called "bottom lines". Bottom lines are essentially rules that you come up with – sometimes with the help of a therapist or sponsor – that make up your abstinence plan.

I once worked with a client who struggled with boundaries when she first started seeing someone. She wanted to see them as much as possible, but this meant that her day-to-day life revolved around when her partner was free. She lived a full life and had a busy job, but that all went out the window if her partner decided they wanted to see her.

We talked about putting in a bottom line when it came to the initial stages of dating someone. This bottom line consisted of meeting them once a week. She felt terrified by the idea that she might have to say no to them. She was afraid they would get bored and reject her. However, by putting in this bottom line, it meant that she felt more in control of her life, and this consequently helped settle her anxiety around the relationship.

Digital Detox

As with other behavioural addictions, abstaining from smartphones or screens is not straightforward. It is likely we will need some sort of screen for work or for staying in communication with others. So how can we abstain from that or achieve a "digital detox"?

Some ideas you can try include:

- **Limiting your use:**
    - Try a digital fast where you abstain from all digital devices for a short period of time, or on a certain day each week.
    - Set an alarm to remind you to take time away from your phone or device to go for a walk, read or engage in another non-digital activity. Some smartphones can set time limits on certain apps.
    - Put your phone on airplane mode when you are exercising to prevent you from accessing social media.
    - Leave your device near the front door when you come home so you do not have it around when you are sitting on the couch or eating.

- **Limiting the technology:**
    - Reduce the capabilities of your phone so that it cannot access apps related to social media and gaming.
    - Uninstall games, apps or functions on your phone or computer which you find particularly addictive.

- **Removing distractions:**
  - Turn off notifications for apps, including social media.
  - Enable the "Do Not Disturb" function when you are at work to prevent messages and notifications.
  - Reduce the frequency of receiving emails to hourly.[13 14]

Creating an Abstinence Plan

So what might abstinence look like for you? First, be honest about which substances or behaviours you need to abstain from. What boundaries or bottom lines can you implement in your life to help break any destructive addictive patterns? Remember that you can gain a lot from a trial abstinence. For example, you could try taking a few months off from social media or online shopping.

YOUR ABSTINENCE PLAN

Open up your journal to a clean page.

1. Identify the behaviour (or behaviours) that you need to stop doing and write them down.
2. Create a list of short-term goals that target the behaviour you have identified (you can always add to this list of small goals when you've achieved this first list!)
3. Write down three bottom lines/boundaries that you will not cross. For example:
   a. I will not buy a vape
   b. I will not engage with people who are in the process of vaping
   c. I will not keep vapes in the house
4. At the bottom of your list from step three, write: "I will contact 'x' if I feel I might break these bottom lines or want to vape".

5 Write down how you might replace this behaviour with a healthier alternative (don't worry if you can't think of any, we are going to discuss this next!)

If you can share your plan with a friend or family member that would be great, just to help with accountability.

While thinking of what abstinence might look like for you, it's important to remember that abstaining from drugs or behaviours is very hard. Having a support system in place can really help, and asking yourself what that might look like will be beneficial. Do you have certain friends or family members that you can ask for extra support at this time? Can you put different activities in your schedule for the next few weeks that are going to be a loving distraction from your drug/behaviour of choice? Looking after yourself is the main priority during the beginning stages of abstinence, so what does that look like for you? Focusing on a better sleep routine? Making home-cooked meals for yourself?

Breaking Old Habits and Forming New Ones

So how can we change our patterns, our behaviours and our routines that support our addictive behaviours? You may have heard of the transtheoretical model of change and its six stages, which explain the process of making a change.[15 16] When thinking about breaking our patterns we only need to think about steps 2, 3 and 4. We will talk about steps 5 and 6 later in the book.

1 **Pre-Contemplation:** We are basically in denial, and we do not consider changing our behaviours. For example, we are currently smoking.

2 **Contemplation**: We begin to think about a change. For example, we can analyse whether the smoking is worth it.
3 **Preparation**: We decide that a change would be a good idea and we start to research tools or ways to help us change. For example, we look up nicotine replacement therapies or find out about local smoking cessation clinics.
4 **Action**: We actively put our plans from our preparation stage into practice. For example, we attend our appointments and take any medication that is recommended.
5 **Maintenance**: We continue our new way of behaving. For example, we continue to attend our appointments.
6 **Relapse**: This doesn't always happen in the cycle, but we may go back to our old ways. For example, we start smoking again.

Now that we know what each stage is, let's look at some techniques throughout the cycle.

Pre-Contemplation and Contemplation Stages

We've talked about denial in its own dedicated chapter (see pages 85–96). But if we are teetering between the pre-contemplation and contemplation stages, being mindful and mapping out our addictive behaviour can be useful. As we have seen, our addictions can be something we do automatically, and so being more aware of the actual experience of our addiction and the negative sensations around their use can be helpful.[17] [18]

Continuing with our smoking example, we might map the following:

- **When do I smoke:** At work. After dinner. Before bed
- **Why do I smoke (the highs of addiction):** It helps me relieve stress and relaxes me. It gives me a regular break at work. I like socializing with people outside.
- **Who do I smoke with:** Colleagues from work

- **What do I not like about smoking (the lows of addiction):** It is expensive. It makes my breath and my clothes smell bad. I feel guilty that it is unhealthy. I am not as fit as I could be and I get breathless when I go for a run.

From this list we can see that we do get benefits from smoking, but this is outweighed by the drawbacks. This can give us the extra, objective motivation we need to consider making a change and move on to the preparation stage.

Preparation Stage

Once we decide to change our behaviour, then we enter the preparation stage. This is where we plan:

1 How we will replace the benefits our addiction gives us.
2 How we will avoid the associated cues that can trigger our addiction.
3 Where we will receive external support.

Mapping our addiction has highlighted the benefits (or highs) that our addiction gives us and identified the needs that our addiction fulfils. It can be helpful to address these needs through alternative routes by forming new, kinder habits to satisfy our needs. Therapy can also be beneficial.

Again using the example of smoking, it's important to find alternative ways to help reduce stress levels as a substitute for smoking. You could research a yoga studio to attend or look into a mindfulness app to download. You could also see a therapist.

Another key part of mapping our habits is identifying environmental or social cues that might trigger our cravings. I advise my clients to plan how they might, where possible, avoid or minimize exposure to these cues. It can be helpful to replace a routine or cue with another to help the transition. For example, you recognize that smoking at work with colleagues gives you a regular break and allows you to socialize. Obviously, you could avoid going out for a break where people are smoking. However, substituting that cue for another would be helpful. For example, you could go for a brief walk around the block when others are going to smoke.

Naturally we need to take responsibility for our actions and not rely on others, but telling friends, colleagues or family members that we want to change could be helpful. This can give us the extra motivation we need and can prepare them for our change in behaviour. Hopefully it will prompt them to be considerate around you or challenge us if we consider repeating the addictive behaviour again. However, making a change is a personal decision, and you should only do this if you feel comfortable. For example, you may tell colleagues at work that you are thinking about stopping smoking. This could prevent them from inviting you to smoking breaks in future or talking about smoking around you.

Finally, we can also research therapists or medical professionals that can help us with our addictive behaviours. For example, you may see your doctor or nurse for advice surrounding nicotine replacement therapy.

Action Stage and Forming New Habits

The action stage is where we put our above plans into action. However, I also want to talk about forming new habits here.

In the preparation stage we talked about finding self-care alternatives to the perceived benefits that our addictive behaviour gives us. This will require us to commit to a new behaviour or routine.

So how do we make a new, healthy habit stick?

1. **Start small:** Remember, we humans fear change! Running ten miles every day may not be realistic, but going for a ten-minute run might be.

2 **Set a regular time or place:** This can help build new cues associated with a routine and can help us stay motivated. For example, "When we are at home, I will have dinner at the same time as my partner each night in the dining room."
3 **Simplify the task during the learning phase:** Instead of starting with "I am going to eat healthily", start with something that requires minimal thinking, such as, "I am going to have granola for breakfast." Although this might reduce variability, in the learning phase of forming a new habit, keeping a simple, repeatable automatic behaviour helps.[19 20 21]
4 **Have a habit buddy:** Starting a habit with a friend might make things easier. It can make the habit more enjoyable, and your friend can also motivate you.[22]
5 **Reward yourself:** Of course, new habits form when you are rewarded! So give yourself some sort of treat each time you stick with it.
6 **Try to find a healthy habit you enjoy:** The change for me really came about with doing new things that integrated the passions I had – creative things that allowed me to get in touch with a part of myself I had locked away for so long. For example, I love singing, and so I joined a choir!

At the start of the chapter, we talked about habits influencing our belief systems and vice versa. Building our own self-care, taking time to look after ourselves and creating healthy habits can help reshape our identity in a positive way.

For example, after my own period of exercise abstinence, my therapist and nutritionist told me that I needed to come up with a new plan that didn't include cardiovascular exercise. Yoga seemed to fit the bill. Although I hated it at first, yoga taught me that if I am persistent at something, then I will see and feel the change. I was never a flexible person, but with time my whole body opened, and I could suddenly do things that had never even crossed my mind. This gave me confidence in myself and made me realize that I didn't need to please others to feel self-worth. This wasn't about anyone else; this was about me. Not only this, but I gained a new-found appreciation for my body and what it is capable of. This really helped quiet down that eating disorder voice inside my head.

It is of course very difficult to learn new habits and change our behaviour, and it requires repetition and dedication. But how long does it take?

In a study done by Phillippa Lally in the *European Journal of Social Psychology*, the process of habit formation in the everyday lives of 96 volunteers was investigated. The researchers analysed the amount of time between each person starting a new behaviour and automatically doing it. The findings were that, on average, it took slightly more than two months.

What was interesting was that "missing one opportunity to perform the behaviour did not materially affect the habit-formation process."[23] To put it simply, it doesn't matter if you make mistakes every now and again – forming a new habit is more about the overall effort, and a few mistakes won't upset the overall change. It's not about getting it perfect. However, I think it's important to mention that, when it comes to abstaining from an addiction, "slipping up" would be classified as a relapse, not a mere mistake in forming a new, healthy habit, and so is obviously not encouraged.

Changing Habits and Patterns in Our Minds

We can also change the patterns and habits of our thought processes. Although this is usually done through therapy, we can also practice changing the habits of the thoughts themselves on our own. One great way of doing this is a gratitude list. Encouraging your mind to think of three to five things you are grateful for every day will help with channelling your thoughts to a grateful place as opposed to an annoyed, resentful or self-loathing place.

PRACTICING GRATITUDE

Write out five things you are grateful for. Ideally this will be every evening before bed, so perhaps keep a journal or empty pad of paper on your bedside table.

It doesn't have to be just for the big stuff. Did a stranger help you today by flashing a smile? Was the sun out today? Did you have a nice conversation with a colleague at work?

Being grateful for all the small things will help us rewire our thoughts to focus more on what has gone well in our day as opposed to what hasn't. Some research indicates that gratitude lists not only help us with appreciating the positive aspects of life, but also create positive social relationships, wellbeing and physical health (particularly relating to sleep and stress).[24]

Shame

Right at the beginning of the book we talked about shame and how this often can be a cause of addiction (see pages 14–17). Addiction specialist Dr Cosmo Duff Gordon suggests that shame can result in "developing a relationship to some type of addictive process or substance".[25]

It's important to consider that many addicts, due to shame-based personalities and a fear of being seen, struggle to build intimate and open relationships (and that's without elements of codependency or love addiction being present).

In my same interview with him, Dr Duff Gordon said "the antidote to shame is acceptance". To free ourselves from shame, we need to accept ourselves and share our shame with others. We need to realize it is okay to be honest in our relationships, and we need to be able to share our true selves with others.

Acceptance includes self-forgiveness. Anyone with an addiction problem will have behaved in ways that are seen as "bad" and done things they are not proud of. For example, I did not like the person I became when I was drunk. I would become loud and boisterous and sometimes be quite nasty to people. I wouldn't always remember these things the next day, and some of the things I said to people came back to haunt me years later. I would beat myself up about my behaviour, even though it had happened years before. I had to challenge myself by being forgiving and being kinder to myself for the ways I had acted or the things I had said that upset people.

SHARING OUR SHAME

Start by writing out the things you feel shame about, getting honest with yourself first and foremost. The second step is to share those things with someone that you feel safe with. In a 12-step recovery process, this would be considered step 4, but you don't have to attend meetings or take part in that specific process to share your own shame. In order to break the same patterns that we have been engaging in for a long time, we need to combat the shame-based fear that we feel if we are going to bring about change.

Connection

So, if accepting and sharing ourselves with others is the key to dissolving our shame, and shame is a key driver in addiction, then we can infer that connection is the antithesis of addiction.

In a famous TED Talk titled "Everything You Think You Know About Addiction Is Wrong", Johann Hari, a British journalist, discusses the research available on the underlying causes of addiction and summarizes that "the opposite of addiction is not sobriety. The opposite of addiction is connection".[26]

So much of the connection we seek today is through a phone, but what we forget is that we are human beings who are used to living in communities and who thrive off personal connection. Even though we are more "connected" than ever – through social media or via our smartphones – we are experiencing less intimacy and less true connection within our relationships.

A very interesting study was conducted in the 1980s by Canadian psychologist Bruce Alexander.[27] This study involved rats being placed in two different cages with morphine water. In one cage there was a large community of rats which, in addition to the morphine water, had an array of other types of stimulation such as hamster wheels, multicoloured balls, plenty of food to eat and spaces for mating and raising litters. They called this the "Rat Park". In the other cage, there were fewer rats and no extra stimulation.

The rats in the smaller cage would get hooked on the morphine and occasionally overdose. However, the rats in the "Rat Park" would avoid the morphine water or consume less. This suggested that addiction is not just about the physical or biological consumption of the drug itself but is also linked to lack of intimate connection.

Something I hear a lot when working with clients who are afraid to let go of their drug/behaviour of choice is that they won't be included as much anymore. They feel a sense of togetherness when drinking, taking drugs or even gaming with their friends. But I challenge the nature of this "togetherness". Is it real connection when we are under the influence? Is using with others really bonding us through intimacy? Or is it just a way to feel like we are keeping up with everyone else? Are we afraid of letting go of a behaviour for fear of missing out?

Breaking my patterns of using with people who no longer served me was probably the biggest catalyst to my change.

That's not to say I didn't have moments of feeling incredibly lonely and frightened, but it meant I was forced to narrow my support network to those people who really cared about me and wanted to help me change.

Have you got any friends or acquaintances who you feel are not contributing positively to your life? If you are afraid of what might happen if you distance yourself from them, it is worth examining the reasons for this fear.

It's also important to consider the expectations we have of other people in response to our change. It can help to bear in mind that everyone will bring their own projections and judgements to our decisions of change, but this doesn't mean that it's not the right thing for us. Not everyone will be excited about us wanting to break the harmful habits in our life, but that says more about them than it does about us. We don't know what our change might trigger in them.

For example, if we tell our best friend that we are going to try to abstain from shopping for a few months, and they themselves have an unhealthy relationship with shopping, we will be acting as a mirror to them. This could be confronting and result in them either getting angry or minimizing our decision.

It can be useful to ask yourself, before engaging in an addictive behaviour with friends, whether you want to engage in it at that time or not. If your friends weren't there, would you have the urge to engage in the behaviour at all?

I want to remind you that you don't have to tell people that you are thinking of making any changes in your life. This is your process, and it simply isn't the business of anyone else unless you decide to disclose that information. I have found over the years that sometimes it is best to wait until you feel more confident about certain changes or new patterns of behaviours before telling other people. This is because my decisions to change were usually met with others' opinions and projections about what they thought I should do according to their own experiences versus what would be the best thing for me.

During my journey of change, the best bit has been finding people who are more of my tribe. Allowing myself to change has created space for new hobbies and people to come into my life, people who enjoy the same things as me – such as yoga or rock climbing – but who also speak my language and are more able to support me.

Change has allowed me to grow as a person, and it has also helped me realize that what I want can change and how I want my life to look can also change. Change is hard, but it's also rewarding, otherwise we wouldn't do it. Annoyingly, the rewards are sometimes not known before the change takes place.

Change is a journey, and sometimes you wonder if you are doing the right thing. But in hindsight, I understand that my addiction had dug me into a hole, and change allowed me to climb my way out.

AFFIRMATIONS

Let's now finish off with something a bit more loving. Take your journal or a piece of paper and write three affirmations – three qualities that you have that you are proud of or that you like about yourself. If you struggle with this, that's okay. It can be helpful to think about someone you love and ask yourself what qualities they have that you like or admire. Can you find the same qualities within yourself? I'll start:

I am kind.

I am funny.

I am trustworthy.

CHAPTER 8
DEALING WITH THE FEELINGS

Feelings – The Good, the Bad and the Ugly

I remember going to see my therapist one day, and I had nothing to say. Nothing had particularly happened that week, I was tired and I didn't want to share anything in particular. I sat there with my arms folded, shrugged and said, "I have nothing to say!"

"That's okay," my therapist replied, "I just want you to close your eyes and tell me if anything comes to mind."

I closed them. Nothing. I started to think about how pointless this all was, how I was wasting his time and that I just needed to stick to my routine. I didn't need therapy really. But then ... I started to cry. This pain, this sense of "life isn't fair", this anger burst out of me. Where did it come from, and why hadn't I felt it before?

I couldn't remember the last time I had sat still. I was always engaging in a routine, seeing friends, keeping busy. If I was at home I would have the television on or be on my phone. I couldn't even go to sleep unless I had *Friends* on in the background!

We have a tendency as humans to try to control how we feel. We chase good feelings and avoid the bad. We might find something to focus on – like running a marathon or staying late at work – to make us feel a sense of achievement, to give us a high or to distract ourselves. Sometimes this can be helpful, other times it can make us slip into addictive behaviours.

As I found out, sitting with myself and my feelings without distraction can be difficult. But it is healthy to sit still and be present. Although we shouldn't ruminate too much on our feelings, allowing ourselves to feel can help us understand our needs. This can help us create self-care strategies and focus on any therapy we might engage with.

Feelings can be difficult to deal with in recovery. If we stop doing something that gives us a high, or something that distracts us from ourselves and our feelings, we will be confronted with feelings that perhaps we didn't really want to be feeling in the first place.

So, let's talk about thoughts and feelings, how they influence the addictive cycle and how we might address this. You might find some of the exercises in this chapter confronting, but trust me, this can be a great opportunity to befriend some of these newer feelings and find acceptance for them. Feelings are not the enemy, and once we accept them for what they are and realize how much they can change from moment to moment, it can be liberating.

What Are Feelings and Emotions, and Is There a Difference?

We all experience emotions, and we all have feelings. However, what we might not know is that feelings and emotions are different. I certainly didn't until my therapist explained it to me!

How I like to explain it to clients is that an emotion is a physical reaction our bodies have to a situation. Feelings then are how are our minds interpret that emotion or what thought we attach to that emotion. Therefore, most of the time we cannot have a feeling without there first being a thought. Feelings are our subjective experience of an emotion, and therefore very individual. Only we know how we are feeling in a specific moment, and it can be very difficult to describe it to others.

For example, two people might have an interview the next day. As a result, their hearts are beating faster, they are slightly sweaty and they feel a slight tightness in the chest. They are experiencing the same emotion about the interview. However, one person may interpret this as "I am going to make a fool of myself. I am so nervous", whereas the other person may think, "I am going to nail this interview. I can't wait!"

As we can see, how we feel affects how we interpret any situation we find ourselves in and therefore determines how we respond to it. As a result, feelings are largely responsible for how we experience and live our lives. Feelings are also a window to our needs, and examining our feelings can help us determine what we need for ourselves from moment to moment.

As we grow up, we develop a tendency to repress our emotions and feelings. This could be due to our brains protecting us from various traumas we experience as we grow, or it could be a result of society's traditionally negative attitude to showing emotion (think "stiff upper lip"). Therefore, identifying our feelings can be challenging as we might not be used to expressing them, and we might not be familiar with all the different ways they can manifest.

Also, because feelings can change so often, sometimes it's hard to pick out exactly what our experience is in any given moment. I like to think of feelings as just energy that flows through us, and I find it fascinating that they are impermanent. They are constantly changing and never stay the same. I personally have experienced many feelings in one go. For example, I have felt anger, stress, fear and also hope all at the same time.

Anger	Sadness	Surprise	Fear	Hopeful	Happy	Excited	Disgust
Frustrated	Loneliness	Shocked	Anxious	Peaceful	Love	Anticipation	Repelled
Insulted	Ashamed	Amazed	Nervous	Grateful	Strong	Interested	Dislike
Upset	Loss	Disappointed	Worried	Accepted	Aroused	Curious	Disapproval
Aggressive	Depressed	Betrayed	Cautious	Trusting	Positive	Stressed	Envious
Critical	Unhappy	Startled	Apprehensive	Calm	Powerful	Motivated	Appalled
Mad	Guilt	Confused	Panicked	Expecting	Ecstatic	Eager	Awful
Enraged	Embarrassed	Astonished	Uneasy	Longing	Generous	Pressured	Judgemental
Hostile	Isolated	Moved	On edge	Blessed	Embracing	Overwhelmed	Contempt
Furious	Abandoned	Stimulated	Distressed	Optimistic	Proud	Impatient	Aversion
Provoked	Empty	Touched	Terrified	Confident	Self-assured	Enthusiastic	Repulsion
Annoyed	Hopeless	Disillusioned	Frightened	Expectant	Playful	Energized	Horror
Irritated	Discouraged	Speechless	Insecure	Assured	Courageous	Passionate	Loathing
Vengeful	Wronged	Delighted	Vulnerable	Encouraged	Inspired	Elevated	Detestation
Spiteful	Sorrow	Awe	Threatened	Bright	Joyful	Animated	Hatred

If addiction is based on using external stimuli to help us with what we need internally, it is important that we understand what we are feeling and identify what our needs are. Therefore, it can be helpful to know the array of different feelings we can experience. I encourage clients to look at a feelings chart (see opposite) when they are struggling to identify which feeling they are experiencing in a certain moment. This can help them make sense of and communicate what they are experiencing.

SEEING THE FEELING

It's time to get out your journal or a blank piece of paper. Now, I am going to warn you that this exercise might feel a bit uncomfortable and weird. I would like you to look at the feelings chart opposite. Which feeling do you find uncomfortable or avoid the most? I want you to think about this feeling and then draw it. What shape is it? What colour does your feeling have? Does it consist of different colours? What form does your feeling have, and does it have a texture?

Once you have drawn and maybe even coloured your feeling, I want you to reflect on how it felt to draw it. Did it feel easy or uncomfortable? Did you find that your mind was critical of your drawing? And finally, looking at your picture, what is your relationship to this feeling? Why might you avoid it?

Often we suppress uncomfortable feelings and over time we find it difficult to sit with them. This exercise will let you engage with that feeling, perhaps see it in a different light and, over time, change your experience with it. Remember we are challenging the idea of a bad feeling. All feelings are trying to tell us something! Next time you encounter this feeling, you may be more comfortable with acknowledging it and listening to what you need.

Thoughts and Feelings

Now that we understand feelings a bit better, let's talk about the importance of thoughts and how they are connected to feelings. What I found most difficult about my addiction is the obsessive nature of the disease.

In 2020, Nature Communications published an article summarizing research on the frequency of human thoughts. It was found that the average person has more than 6,000 thoughts a day.[1] This number will obviously differ from individual to individual. I was told in treatment that, in comparison, the addict has roughly the same four thoughts between 12,000 to 60,000 times a day.

Whether that is true or not, I do not know! But when I heard this estimate, I suddenly felt understood. I felt constantly out of control as my thoughts and feelings could never be switched off. My mind was whirring around and around having the same thoughts over and over, making me stuck in an obsessive cycle. The feelings would match, and I would continually sit in this seriously uncomfortable state. Only during the times I was using drink/drugs/food would I be able to arrest those thoughts and experience a state of numbness. As you can imagine, for someone with the same four thoughts 12,000 to 60,000 times a day, it felt like a huge relief to have my mind quietened.

I used to believe that there was something wrong with me or that no one else could possibly understand the way my mind worked. When I was first told by Dr Cosmo Duff Gordon that I was an addict, I did not believe it. But when I started to understand that this was an illness of the mind, it made so much sense to me, and for the first time, I felt like I wasn't the only one.

An important part of my recovery has been getting used to or becoming familiar with feelings that I don't necessarily like. Addicts are generally known to be more sensitive to their feelings: they feel more intensely and can be overwhelmed with emotion, which certainly rings true for me.[2] Before I came into recovery, I didn't like who I was when I was feeling, but I think, in hindsight, it was more that I didn't know how to manage my feelings. I didn't know how to sit with uncomfortable feelings or soothe myself. I always felt the need to change them.

Good Versus Bad Feelings

Feelings and emotions are crucial for our survival. They allow us to interpret the world and our surroundings, which helps us recognize danger and stay safe. For example, feeling frightened of a tiger who is chasing us will give us a better chance of getting away. Therefore, feelings should not be something we fear!

Feelings also enable us to appreciate beauty and build lasting connections with others. As humans, we are inclined to search for the good feelings and avoid the bad feelings. But what do we deem good feelings? Generally, I think we associate good feelings with being comfortable or excited – for example, when we experience contentment, joy or happiness. We also tend to try to avoid or quieten bad feelings such as anger, sadness or loneliness.

I think it's important that we try to change that narrative. What I focus on a lot with my clients is the notion that there are no bad feelings. For example, sadness isn't bad, loneliness isn't bad – these are just two of the many feelings we experience as human beings.

The bad feelings are all experiences that can teach us something – they only become bad when we attach a meaning to them. If we do this, it gives our experience of the feeling more meaning, and we can find it hard to distinguish between the feeling we are having and the reality of certain situations.

Let's go back to the person you saw across the street who didn't wave at you. After one day you might start to feel anxious because you think that they ignored you or you might have done something to upset them. The feeling of anxiety exists because that person didn't wave at you. Anxiety has a habit of verifying our worrying thoughts and making us believe our fears are a reality. Because we now have a feeling connected to a thought, we believe the thought to be real.

That doesn't mean to say that when we have feelings such as anxiety our experience of the feelings isn't real or we haven't been triggered by a situation. Just because we have a certain feeling, it doesn't make our narratives or stories true.

We are also not in control of our feelings, nor can we control how and when they might change. So, when we have an uncomfortable feeling, it might make us feel out of control. When we are in a painful place, we forget that all feelings change. Conversely, when we are experiencing joy or happiness, we never want these feelings to end – yet another reason why we seek external things to keep our levels of dopamine up! However, all things must pass.

Some of us were taught as children that certain feelings were bad or that we shouldn't express our feelings. This means that some of us will find it harder to regulate these feelings or even express them as we get older. For example, if we have been told off for crying or have been told to always smile, these narratives influence what we believe our feelings should be and how we should or shouldn't express them. These narratives can be quite damaging, because it's unrealistic to suggest that we are only ever going to be happy, or that we are never going to be sad. This reinforces the idea that we should always chase feelings of happiness while burying or avoiding negative feelings. This has two effects. First, it encourages a society of chasing highs and being stimulated ("If it feels good, do it!"). Second, it means we become less emotionally aware. We do not listen to our feelings of anxiety, anger or fear and do not pay attention to the needs that these feelings highlight. We become conditioned to look only at the external and not pay attention to the internal.

Feelings and the Addictive Cycle

If we do not know when these uncomfortable feelings are going to end, it is logical that we might look to change how we feel. If we want to experience good feelings, then we may act in a way that gives us a dopamine hit. For example, taking substances such as cocaine or MDMA. We may also act in a way that means we avoid the bad feelings. For example, heroin not only gives the user a rush, but can also provide an escape from their troubles. As Gabor Maté so eloquently puts it, "The wondrous power of a drug is to offer the addict protection from pain while at the same time enabling her to engage the world with excitement and meaning".[3]

Similarly, the release of dopamine that we get when engaging in certain addictive behaviours can numb us from other feelings. Therefore, if we've had a bad day, feel low or just want to change the way we feel, we will turn to something that releases dopamine, like social media. Unlike with addictive substances, it is not always clear to us with behavioural addictions that we are engaging in a repeated, addictive behaviour to take us away from our present feelings. And it is more complicated than just avoiding the bad feelings and chasing the good feelings. I mean, some people who have addictions often feel lousy after they engage in their behaviour of choice, so they must want to avoid that too.

Take, for example, a client of mine who suffers from a spending addiction. We were talking about the feelings that she experiences within the cycle of her addictive behaviour. She usually has a big high when she is looking at clothes or beauty products she wants to buy online. The high continues while she is waiting for the goods to be delivered, but once they arrive, she experiences a sense of apathy and loses interest in what she has ordered almost immediately. Following this, she gives herself a hard time for having spent so much money and thus feels frustrated. She then experiences, as she describes it, a huge sense of emptiness and nothingness. These feelings then lead to her going back online to shopping some more.

We can identify that her high doesn't last forever and her feelings within this cycle are not all pleasant feelings. In fact, she knows she will feel significantly frustrated, empty and low.

After challenging these behaviours together, we explored what she felt after she had abstained from shopping for a few days. She found feelings of failure come to the surface. She felt she had really let herself down by not being where she wanted to be in her life. This was incredibly overwhelming and frightening and was so uncomfortable that she told me she preferred to be back in the addictive shopping cycle than in this place of feeling that she wasn't good enough. At least she got a small high out of what she was doing as opposed to sitting with the newer feelings.

There is an expression that I always use when working with clients: "We would rather be right than happy". In other words, we are inclined to confirm the familiar narratives in our head that make us feel a certain way rather than try to find freedom from the cycle and be happy. Because if the feelings were to be different, they would feel unfamiliar – we wouldn't know where they came from or when they would stop, and hence we might feel out of control.

Are there patterns of behaviour that you engage in knowing full well how you will feel at the end? What feelings might you be avoiding by staying in these cycles? What would it feel like to challenge the behaviours?

Why Do We Fear Sitting Still With Ourselves?

I had spent so many years avoiding any kind of feelings, that when I got clean, I started to experience a lot of them in one go. Suddenly I had to deal with a whole array of feelings: fear, guilt, loneliness. These feelings could be intense. After a few weeks of being sober, I was travelling to a therapy session and suffered a panic attack, for the first time, on the train. I thought I was having a heart attack!

Now I'm going to talk to you about something else I experienced, something significant that you might not think is very problematic: I started to feel bored. During the early stages of my recovery, I had a constant itchy need to distract myself. If I didn't keep busy, I would get bored.

Why might recovery initially feel boring? Well, we start to feel everything we have been avoiding. I believe boredom is a discomfort of being with ourselves. But I don't think this discomfort is restricted to those in recovery. I think a lot of us do not like to sit with ourselves.

Dr Cosmo Duff Gordon noticed an increase in addiction or addictive behaviours during the height of the COVID-19 pandemic.[4] And in the early stages of the pandemic (June 2020), the Centers for Disease Control and Prevention reported that 13 per cent of American adults started using substances as a way of coping.[5]

The question is: did lockdown make new addicts? Potentially. Of course, lockdown was an extremely distressful time for a lot of people. However, Dr Gordon thinks a proportion of these people were already addicts, but there were situational controls in place, such as going to the office. When they were working from home, these controls were then removed. These addictions were probably already there, but during lockdown, the wheels fell off.

So why did the wheels fall off? I think it's because we were forced to – perhaps for the first time – be still with ourselves more than ever before. All those feelings we might have previously buried or avoided came to the surface, and this is what makes sitting still with ourselves so difficult.

So, if repeating addictive behaviour is a way of controlling how we feel or numbing us from uncomfortable feelings, how do we get comfortable with these uncomfortable feelings in the first place? Naturally, we won't always be comfortable with them – we all go through difficult periods in our lives. However, we can at least try to understand that these periods and these feelings come and go. We do not always need to control them or drown them out. Sitting still with ourselves and noticing feelings is okay.

So what do I mean by sitting still? When I say this, I do not necessarily mean sitting on the sofa in silence twiddling your thumbs. Although that would be an example! Sitting still means sitting with yourself or with your feelings. It means refraining from distracting yourself with outside noise and not drowning out your thoughts with something else. This can look different for different people, but it could be sitting in meditation, doing some colouring or completing a puzzle.

I challenge my clients to cook without background noise or start the first 20 minutes of the commute in silence instead of putting on a podcast. Do you ever find yourself on your phone while you are watching TV? If so, sitting still might initially be putting your phone down and watching a film.

Take, for example, my client S. She has a highly stressful, high-powered job and is used to constantly running around from meeting to meeting and working weekends. She doesn't consider downtime or sitting quietly on the weekend as valuable time spent.

I challenged her to book some relaxation time, watch Netflix for a few hours and note what feelings arose. She had a lot of resistance to even sitting down in the first place, and her mind always found things that were "more important" to do.

It took a few weeks, but eventually on a Sunday evening, she found some time to sit still. Once she got beyond the feelings of "This is so pointless", she felt prominent feelings of loneliness and unworthiness. She felt sad and even felt the urge to message an ex-partner to get some validation. She didn't send the text and woke up the next morning with a clear head and some relief.

We explored these feelings of unworthiness and her perception of what she should be achieving. Ultimately, these stemmed from childhood and her need of approval from her parents, which only came from academic achievement.

SITTING WITH SELF

So, let's take it back to you. Take a moment to sit with yourself, and then come back and reflect on your experience with the below questions.

First, identify what you were itching to do to avoid sitting still? Do you reach immediately for your phone in moments of silence? Do you always listen to background noise when you are on your own at home? After a few moments of silence, where does your mind turn to?

Have you ever made plans that got cancelled and then felt uncomfortable that you were left with nothing to do? Did you find yourself quickly trying to fill that time with another plan because you wanted to avoid sitting on your own at home?

What are the feelings you might be avoiding in such situations? What does your version of sitting with yourself look like?

Write down some of your observations in your journal. You can add to this next time you sit with yourself and notice a different thought or distraction creeping in.

Breaking the Thought Patterns

Doing things that are different to your usual routine might feel weird or uncomfortable, but I would challenge you to try it. Going out of your comfort zone is the first step in breaking the usual patterns we find ourselves in. The reason we are comfortable is because we distract ourselves!

In today's fast-paced society, a lot of us feel the need to constantly work toward a goal, to achieve something. I say sitting still is a perfectly valid goal, and listening to your mind is an achievement.

Therefore, I encourage you to do more things in silence. Try to leave your phone at home when you go for a run or for a walk. Try not to listen to podcasts or music when you cook. You may be surprised what feelings come to the surface when you're not distracted by outside noise, and reflecting on these feelings is an important step toward breaking thought patterns that don't serve you.

To go one step further, I encourage you to be creative in your sitting still. Being creative, in whatever form, can be confronting. If we usually avoid our feelings, expressing ourselves creatively might seem very alien. If we tend toward perfectionism, producing a piece of art that doesn't look "right" or "perfect" can feel pointless or uncomfortable.

VISUALIZATION

Now we are going to try a visualization exercise to evoke feelings while being still and getting creative.

I want you to think back to a time in your life when you were younger. Perhaps between the ages of 8 and 12. Can you see yourself at that age? What were you wearing? Where were you?

I then want you to think about a scenario at that age when you were distressed, when you felt sad or frustrated, alone or angry – the first scenario that comes into your mind. What happened? Where were you and who was with you?

I want you to get out a piece of blank paper and draw that scenario to the best of your ability. This isn't about creating an amazing piece of art; there is no right or wrong. You can get as messy as you like with it. It can be just shapes if you like, as long as it represents the scenario for you. Make sure you draw yourself within this scenario. Were you sitting down or standing up? Were you on your own?

Once you have drawn this, I want you to look at the image in front of you. Take a minute for yourself. What do you feel? Are you noticing any initial judgemental thoughts about the drawing you have produced? Can you put those to one side and remember the feelings you had at this distressing moment?

Next, I want you to draw your adult self, as you are today, in the same image. Draw yourself in a way that illustrates you comforting your younger distressed self. Do you have your arm around them? Are you giving them a hug? Can you think of what you would say to them that they needed to hear at that time?

Close your eyes and take a moment to stay with your younger self. Stay with the feelings of distress and notice how you comfort them. How does that feel for you today? Do you feel compassion for your younger self, or do you not feel connected to that person?

There is no right or wrong answer. But if you struggle to connect to that younger version of you, I suggest digging up some old photos of you as a kid. Maybe set them as your desktop background or stick them on your fridge. You could also imagine your younger self with you for the next week – when you go to work, when you are watching TV on the sofa. Imagine looking after them and try to access some of the feelings that they might have been experiencing.

Mindfulness

Okay, so we've sat with ourselves, and all these feelings are coming out. Some of these feelings aren't nice. What do we do with them?

Well, it can be helpful to discuss these feelings with a therapist, and we will talk about the different kinds of therapy in the next chapter. However, let's focus on what we should do when we get these feelings.

In truth, I don't want you to do anything! I just want you to *notice* what feelings you are getting. Simply be mindful.

We've seen throughout the book how the past influences how we see the present. We've seen that our belief systems, our defence mechanisms, our identities and our thoughts are built on our past – our upbringing, events in our lives, relationships we have nurtured, shame we have carried. These feed into our thoughts and feelings and influence how we interpret our current situation and surroundings. Mindfulness allows us to reclaim the present.

Mindfulness is a concept that has been around for 2,500 years, originating on the Indian subcontinent.[6] It has been increasingly applied in psychotherapy following the work of Professor Jon Kabat-Zinn around 40 years ago.

When we are practicing mindfulness, we focus on the present moment: where we are, what we are doing, our bodies and our sensations. We allow any thoughts or feelings to enter our minds, but instead of dwelling on them, we let those feelings float away like clouds. This trains our brains to embrace the reality of things and detach our thoughts from what our bodies are actually experiencing.[7]

Mindfulness can be practiced anywhere and can be practiced in whatever way you choose to "sit still". However, it can also be achieved through meditation or through breath awareness.

MEDITATION

First, find somewhere comfortable to sit and, if you prefer, close your eyes. Next, pay attention to your breathing:

the sensation in your nose or mouth, the rising and falling of your chest and the sound of the air moving in and out. If a thought comes into your head, that's fine, but then try to let the thought go. Do not beat yourself up if you do get attached to thoughts or ideas. As soon as you notice yourself dwelling on a particular thought, let that thought go and then focus on your breathing again.

With time, learning to be present, being aware of our thoughts and feelings, and not judging them can reduce the control they have over us. To help achieve this, Professor Kabat-Zinn recommends nine attitudes to cultivate when we are being mindful in our daily lives.[8] [9] [10]

1 **Don't judge:** Often we have an opinion on our thoughts or our experiences ("I like this", "I hate this", etc.). Try to be mindful when this happens and not judge your judging! Eventually, we will begin to see that our judging is often very bleak and we are naturally quick to judge. Over time, we can learn to be more open-minded and accepting.
2 **Be patient:** Often we look past what is happening now and focus on the next important event. Being patient means we can live in the current moment.
3 **Beginner's mind:** Try to encounter each moment as if you have experienced it for the first time. If we are familiar with an experience, we bring with it our preconceived opinions. Be open to all possibilities. We may have eaten the same sandwich as yesterday, but it is the first time we are experiencing *that* sandwich!
4 **Trust yourself:** The more we trust ourselves, the more we can trust our relationships and how we will deal with challenges in the future.
5 **Do not strive:** We are used to constantly trying to achieve something. Mindfulness is a way of practicing non-doing.

It doesn't require you to achieve something, and the thoughts do not need to go anywhere. The goal is to be in that moment.

6. **Accept things as they are:** We are not present if we keep thinking of ways that our present could be improved.
7. **Let go:** Try to let all thoughts come and go. Try not to cling on to an idea or force yourself to feel a certain way. Letting be is also a way of letting go.

There are plenty of ways to practice mindfulness, and guided meditations are available on YouTube and through smartphone apps such as Headspace. Have a look and see what works for you.

Try to think of a time and place where you can be mindful. Remember, this doesn't necessarily have to be at home. You can practice mindful eating where you are more aware of the food's taste and textures, or you can take in the sights and sounds around you when you go for a walk.[11]

Withdrawal and Cravings

Another cause of boredom in early recovery is withdrawal. Our bodies become deprived of that regular spike of dopamine, which can lead to dysphoria – a state of constant dissatisfaction. A lot of the work of recovery involves perseverance and trusting that our bodies will adapt and our brains will reach homoeostasis and be satisfied with more consistent levels of dopamine that are associated with everyday life. It is very hard to trust that the negative feelings of withdrawal will change and we will start to experience happiness again, but for it to happen, we must remain abstinent.

Everyone's withdrawal will be different and will depend on our behaviour or substance of choice. In the initial stages of abstinence, we might experience anxiety, irritability, insomnia, dysphoria and cravings.

We've also talked about how our brains make us crave our addiction. Some cravings manifest physically if we are addicted to a substance. This can include sweating, palpitations, anxiety and nausea. It's important for me to reiterate that those withdrawing from physically addictive substances such as heroin, crystal meth and alcohol need their withdrawal period to be conducted in a safe and monitored environment under medical supervision. Always speak to a medical professional before stopping a physical substance.

But now let's talk more about emotional cravings. These can manifest as feelings of anxiety, fears of separation from our addictive behaviour or intrusive thoughts. Of course, these can be exacerbated by the new and uncomfortable feelings that might arise now that we are not distracting ourselves.

Let's think about our phones for a minute. Statistics vary across the world, but one study suggests that 6.3 per cent of Americans are addicted to their smartphone.[12] Additionally, in one survey conducted in America, 57 per cent of the participants self-reported smartphone addiction,[13] while a survey of Chinese medical students showed that 52.8 per cent felt they were addicted.[14] I think it is something a lot of us might be familiar with.

I definitely have addictive behaviours around my phone. When it is not on my person I sometimes have anxiety and panic when I reach for it and it's not there. Picking up my phone automatically, wherever I am – walking down the street or first thing in the morning – is undeniably a means of distraction for me, and it's something I am very rarely without. When it is not with me, I experience unpleasant feelings of craving my phone. I might also experience intrusive thoughts such as "Someone might be trying to get hold of me" or "Have I missed an important email?"

Using your smartphone as an example, do you feel a sudden panic if you're not near it? If your internet or social media is down, do you find yourself feeling annoyed, sad, frustrated?

I remember being told while I was in treatment for my eating disorder that emotional cravings tend to last about 15 to 40 minutes (physical cravings can last much longer).[15] In the moment we fear that our feelings of unease will never go away – but remember, the craving will fade with time.

But how do we deal with these cravings? Well, when we get a craving it is best to distract ourselves in a loving way. For example, there is evidence that going for a 15-minute walk can reduce cravings for a high-calorie sugary snack.[16] Alternatively, you can call a friend to talk about the feelings you're experiencing or even just talk to them about the rest of your day. You could also take out a colouring book or even do a puzzle. Taking our mind off the craving can help the feelings subside, and once they do, you'll be left with a feeling of pride and accomplishment.

It's true that cravings can be so intense at times that we feel like if we don't pick up, we will never feel okay again. Not only this, during abstinence our cravings may also be accompanied by thoughts and feelings we have been avoiding. But being mindful of our thoughts and feelings and letting them wash over us will help. The cravings and the feelings will pass.

One of my favourite quotes about feelings comes from Jonatan Martensson: "Feelings are much like waves, we can't stop them from coming, but we can choose which ones to surf." This perfectly sums up my experience of feelings today. I experience feelings all the time. Like waves, they keep coming, no matter where I am or what the circumstances. But slowly learning how to not react to them, or act out on them, has helped me create space between myself and harming myself due to an uncomfortable feeling. Being aware and mindful of what we are feeling can help us surf, but it can also be a platform for therapy. Let's talk about that and other people who can help with your recovery.

CHAPTER 9
SEEKING HELP AND RECOVERY

Planting the Seed of Recovery

In September 2024, I will be ten years clean, sober and abstinent. That is something I never thought was possible. I also never expected recovery to be such a huge part of my life. I guess I never thought freedom was possible. Freedom not just from the addictive behaviours, but also from the self-loathing and worthlessness I had felt for so many years.

I feel compelled to let you know that my recovery is not perfect. It never has been, and it never will be. I am not saying this to give myself a hard time, I'm saying this to let you know that the recovery journey can be messy. It's complicated, uncomfortable and murky at times.

When thinking of recovery, especially early recovery, I like to use the analogy of a seed. A seed that gets planted in dark soil. This little seed has no idea when it is going to reach the surface of the soil and get to the light it needs to thrive. However, it keeps going despite not knowing and pushes through the dark until finally it gets to where it needs to be.

We've seen how the seed can sprout through abstinence, breaking habits and being mindful of our thoughts. But the sprout can also be guided to the light by either outpatient or inpatient treatment. Not everyone can obtain abstinence on their own or through weekly therapy sessions. As I have mentioned, some people need to detox in a safe, medical environment as doing it on their own at home can be very dangerous.

Needing extra support isn't a failure. For some of us it's the most loving thing and can help us fully surrender. I believed for a while that to go into treatment meant I was weak. It meant that I didn't have control over my life, and I felt ashamed. But today, I can wholeheartedly say it saved my life in more ways than one. Obviously, it helped me abstain from destructive behaviours, but it also helped me realize that there was a life outside of using and starving myself. It helped me connect with other people who could relate to my feelings, and for the first time, I didn't feel alone.

For me, it was a combination of self-care, help from friends and family, encouragement from a sponsor (an addict in recovery) and the guidance of a professional therapist. Let's look at these different ways of getting support.

Seeking Help from Friends and Family

I know the term "reaching out" gets thrown around a lot these days, but it's definitely easier said than done. Especially if we are reaching out to those in our lives who don't understand what we mean when we say "abstinence" or "recovery".

So, how do we do it? What do we say?

Some of my clients ask me questions like "How can I reach out to someone without going into all the details?" or "What if I don't want to disclose my recovery journey but I need to talk to someone about how I'm feeling?"

There is no right or wrong answer. How we address our recovery with people who don't necessarily understand is very individual, and some of us will find it easier than others to ask for help. I think the main thing comes down to what you need in that moment. In my opinion, asking for our needs to be met and asking for help are the same thing.

Let's use spending addiction as an example. Picture the scene: you've had a long and stressful day. You come home and all you want to do is browse online to help you relax. You know that it will make you feel numb, and that feels like the easiest thing to do, but you know it is not necessarily the most loving thing for you as you are trying to abstain from this behaviour.

Think about what you need in that moment. You may need a friend to come over and hang out to give you a positive distraction from the craving. You may need a family member to listen to your stressful day, or you may need your partner to make sure dinner is ready when you get home. Once you understand what you need, you will have to learn to ask for it. This can be the scary part.

So why might you be afraid to ask for what you need? If you are not used to having your needs met, it makes sense that suddenly asking for it could feel daunting and unfamiliar. For example, if, as a child, you needed more hugs from a parent or caregiver but were told no, your emotional needs were not met. Therefore, you may have shut down the part of you that asks for help – you may have gotten used to meeting your own needs.

Asking for our needs to be met makes us vulnerable. This can of course feel risky. To ask for a need to be met means we could be rejected. When we are entering into recovery, trying new things and having new feelings, we are already vulnerable. So, the fear of rejection can be more heightened than usual.

Sometimes your friends or family might not react in the way that you need them to. They might not understand what is going on for you emotionally, and trust me, I know that's frustrating and can feel really lonely at times. As we have seen, our family and friends may use our addiction to distract them from their own problems, or they might be in denial themselves. Sometimes the denial can be just about the fact that you're struggling. That denial can make it difficult to ask them for help.

Our role in the family can also act as a barrier and feed into our family's denial. For example, let's say your role in your family has been the peacekeeper, or the one who has always been self-sufficient. If you suddenly start asking for your needs to be met, that won't necessarily fit in with the idea of who your family need you to be. This may result in them finding it hard to meet your needs or simply ignoring you.

If you are struggling to get through to a family member by asking for help, try to remind yourself it's not your fault. They might not be capable of giving you their help. But that doesn't mean you don't deserve help and support.

Therefore, it can be helpful to look for support outside of your social circle. A turning point for me was when I engaged in talking therapy – by myself and in a group – and began attending AA meetings. Talking things through with a professional or with people who are going through similar experiences can make reaching for help much easier.

12-Step Fellowships

My recovery journey would not have been the same without the 12-step fellowship. These fellowships do not just include Alcoholics Anonymous or Narcotics Anonymous. These days, there is pretty much a 12-step fellowship for any addictive behaviour: GAA (Gaming Addicts Anonymous), DA (Debtors Anonymous), OA (Overeaters Anonymous), CA (Cocaine Anonymous) and so on. Now, while these 12-step fellowships aren't everyone's cup of tea, they certainly helped me and enabled me to find connection with other people who were going through similar things.

Alcoholics Anonymous was founded in 1935 in Ohio by Bill W, a New York stockbroker, and Dr Bob S, a surgeon, who were both alcoholics. Before they met, Bill had managed to get sober while Bob had struggled to do so. However, when they were introduced, Bob found himself face to face with a fellow sufferer who had managed to get better. A key part of Bob's recovery was Bill explaining to him that alcoholism was a spiritual illness or a malady of mind, emotions and body. They then created Alcoholic Anonymous, which continues to help millions of alcoholics and addicts recover today.[1]

You might wonder how joining a group such as AA could help you. Well, as we have discussed previously, connection is the antithesis of addiction. Most addicts are seeking connection, love and a sense of belonging. After years of feeling like I didn't fit in anywhere, when I began attending meetings, I felt that the people there were speaking my language. Not just because we all had similar relationships to drugs and alcohol, but because every person that spoke felt the same way I did: empty. It was the emptiness I had inside that drove me toward addictive behaviours.

This is why the founders of AA considered addiction itself not so much a medical illness, but a spiritual one. Yes, we might be physically addicted to a substance, but what got us turning to the substance in the first place are those feelings within ourselves we are trying to escape from. Following a relatively short medical detox, often the primary treatment for substance abuse is a 12-step spiritual programme.

So how does the 12-step fellowship programme work? How has it helped millions of people recover and abstain from their drug or behaviour of choice? The fellowship is based on social interactions. Not only do you get emotional peer support, but you also learn from people's experience of recovery and can learn practical tips on how to manage your addictive behaviour. Once you build relationships in recovery and your life revolves more around recovery-based activities and meetings, there is a responsibility not only to yourself, but to your sponsor and the fellowship as a whole. This can be a great help in preventing relapse.

For example, in the times I felt the urge to drink, I played the tape forward and would think about having to tell my AA peers that I had lapsed. Now, that's not to say that if you ever relapse, you're not welcomed back in with open arms, because that is always what happens. But the anticipation of the shame I would feel if that happened was enough to keep me from picking up a drink.

The 12-step fellowship works with positive reinforcement. Every time you reach a certain milestone of abstinence – for example, 30 days – you are given a chip. Everyone is there to clap for you while you pick up your chip at the end of the meeting. The most important chip given is the one that is for the newcomer – the person at their very first meeting who doesn't even have to be clean to pick it up. It's symbolic of surrendering, making a different choice and taking the first step in coming to meetings. Picking up my chips was definitely a relapse-deterrent for me. I remember so clearly picking up my 60-day chip; I had a sense of pride and achievement that I don't think I had ever felt.

SMART Recovery

So, following on from talking about 12-step fellowships, I want to make it very clear that 12-step recovery isn't for everyone. For example, some people find the spiritual element of the Anonymous fellowships difficult to relate to. Yes, it has been proven to work for millions of people, but you might not be one of them, and that's okay. There isn't just one road to recovery.

This is where SMART Recovery comes into play. SMART stands for Self-Management and Recovery Training. It is a programme that provides training and education for people who are looking to change their problematic behaviours such as addiction. They cover not only alcohol and drugs but also addictions to the internet, shopping, gambling, food and cigarettes.

What makes SMART different? Well, they strongly believe that everyone has a personal choice and the power to change harmful and strongly engrained habits. SMART is secular and is based on various therapeutic techniques, including cognitive behavioural therapy (CBT), which we talked about previously.

The SMART approach is built around four main points:

1 **Motives and goals:** SMART Recovery aims to demonstrate that addictive behaviours might be effective in the short term but not in the long term when we use them to meet primary human goals: to survive, to be happy and to avoid pain.
2 **Beliefs:** The approach looks to identify your belief systems, analyse them and alter them.
3 **Emotions:** SMART Recovery looks to help people cope with their emotions and increase self-acceptance.
4 **Behaviours:** It encourages the breaking of old patterns and replacing these addictive habits with new ones.

SMART Recovery promotes the idea that we are all individuals, and we need to find out what works best for us. We can do this via a "toolbox" of methods that is taught in the programme via professionals.[2]

Meetings are easy to access online or in person, and they have workbooks you can use to help you on your journey.

One technique I find particularly helpful is the ABC tool (Action, Beliefs, Consequences). This tool tries to free you from the negative effects of your own thinking. For example, you may say to someone "You made me angry". In reality, that is not strictly true. The other person hasn't made you angry – it is actually the way they have behaved that has made you angry. Your anger is based on your assumption that the other person should act in the way that you want them to.

Let's say someone hasn't thanked us when we let them in front of us in traffic. We don't really have any control over whether they thank us or not. Therefore, it would probably be easier for us if we don't get angry about it or let it ruin our day.

If we believe that everyone on the road must thank us and they do not, then we will want to do something about it. Since we cannot realistically control what other people do, this often makes us feel angry or upset. Changing our thinking from a must ("They must thank me") to a preference ("I would prefer it if they thanked me") can help us be more rational.

The ABC exercise helps people analyse a situation and change their thinking around it without trying to control the external factors that are out of their control.[3] This should make us feel better about similar situations in the future. This can help us with our addictive urges by training us to react more calmly:

- **A**ction: That person didn't thank me when I let them into my lane.
- **B**eliefs about the action: They must thank someone who has let them through.
- **C**onsequences of your beliefs: I feel very angry, and I resent that person. I don't stop thinking about it until I get home, and I feel I have to have a cigarette to calm down.
- **D**ispute your beliefs: Why should they need to thank me? We all are going the same way. Is it a law? No.
- **E**ffective new belief: It might be polite to say thank you, but ultimately, I have just let him change lanes. Other people let me pass into their lane. I choose not to be angry about it.

If you prefer a more scientific or practical way of recovery, this might be more useful for you. SMART Recovery generally focuses on the present and setting goals for the future instead of looking at the past. There are still meetings, there is still support and I know many people who have found this approach effective.

Now let's look at more psychodynamic approaches and how we can look at the past to understand our belief systems.

Individual Therapy

We've been referring to it throughout the book, but now we will finally talk about that word: therapy. This word may make you curious or it may make you wince. Obviously, as a therapist, I always encourage people to try therapy. Some of you may never have had it before, or you might have tried it a few times but never really found the right therapist for you. What I have come across often is the notion of "I should only be in therapy if I have a problem".

Some of us might think of therapy in terms of going for a few sessions, talking about our immediate pressing issues and then feeling like the work is done and we can get on with our lives. While I understand where that concept has come from, I by no means think it should be the case.

True, engaging in therapy at all, even if it's to explore a certain issue or feeling, can only be beneficial. But for me, the therapy really lies in the therapeutic relationship, the relationship between the therapist and the client – that is where a lot of the healing takes place.

The therapist should always show up for you, no matter what mood you are in. It helps you to show feelings to the therapist that you are afraid of showing to other people, such as sadness, fear or anger. The therapist should accept you no matter what state you find yourself in. The sessions are *your* time. No one else's. So, if you are not used to prioritizing yourself, this can be a challenge.

There is no other relationship in our lives that has the same boundaries or takes the same form as a therapist/client relationship. The therapeutic relationship helps us learn how to accept ourselves with all our vulnerabilities, as well as helping us learn to trust.

This trust can be so important at times we feel we've reached a roadblock in our therapy. This is a time we really need to stick with it. A trusted therapist can help us delve deeper under the surface and perhaps face things we have been avoiding.

Sometimes therapy is boring, or you're convinced your therapist is bored. You may talk about the same things week after week, and nothing seems to be changing. But unpacking all the junk built up in your subconscious takes hard work and time, and it's often not fun. However, it is totally worthwhile.

Therapy is a journey, and it doesn't necessarily have an endpoint. But it is the discoveries, the acceptance and the hope that we experience along the way that can make a real difference.

There are many different options for therapy, especially if you are on a budget. I've included some great links in the Further Resources section on page 185.

Group Therapy

Group therapy – an experience of being vulnerable and open with other people – was also something that I found to be very healing. It also helped validate my own experiences as other members of the group fed back. However, at times this could be confronting. This was mainly because the group was acting as my mirror. I realized that character traits I found annoying in others usually pointed to something about myself that I didn't like. Psychologist Carl Jung called this "psychological projection". To put it simply, we criticize or dislike something about someone else, usually because we hold the same or similar traits. This can be very confronting to acknowledge but really helps with learning to accept ourselves fully, just as we are.

SHINING LIGHT ON YOUR SHADOW

As a quick exercise, I want you to think about someone in your life that irritates you. What is it about them that gets under your skin? I want you to think about this quality and ask yourself: Do I also possess this quality? Is it something that I don't like about myself? Is it a part of myself that I am ashamed of?

This exercise isn't about demonizing anyone, but more about being honest with ourselves. The good news about acknowledging parts of ourselves that we don't like – which Carl Jung called the "shadow" – is that we are able to start accepting all of who we are, not just bits that we deem "good enough" or bits that we have been conditioned to show more of.

Have a look near you and see if you can find a group therapy session. Sometimes simply typing "group therapy near me" into Google can yield plenty of options. You don't have to be in treatment to attend group therapy. It might be daunting to walk into a room full of strangers and be open and vulnerable, but it can certainly teach you a lot about yourself.

Experiential Therapies

Experiential therapy can be another useful tool under the therapeutic umbrella that can help with a wide range of life challenges, including eating disorders and addictive behaviours. It is an approach to psychotherapy that involves physical activities and immersive tools to help you explore painful feelings and difficult situations. Some examples of experiential therapies are psychodrama, art therapy and music therapy.

Psychodrama

Psychodrama is a form of experiential therapy that might feel more uncomfortable for some. Psychodrama usually happens within groups, but it can also be practiced in a personal one-on-one setting.

I had a conversation with Rebecca McGurrell MBACP/BPA, a therapist who advocates for psychodrama.[4] I asked her about the benefits of this type of therapy and how it differs from usual psychotherapy.

In a psychodrama session, you can practise complex dynamics with other people. For example, you can practise being angry in a safe space. In our lives we might have fears such as, "I can't risk being angry at someone because they might reject me", but in this setting you get to practise it! The classical session runs during a two-and-a-half-hour period which allows people to warm up to the space, the director and each other. By practising and acting out these scenarios, the ability to effectively express your emotions will eventually seep into your unconscious. Psychodrama provides the opportunity to come out of your own head and speak to parts of yourself that you've perhaps struggled to access.

Psychodrama also allows participants to set up a scenario to do reparative work using props. For example, if we think of a time when we were mistreated as a child, we can imagine we are now talking to the person who mistreated us, we can tell them they were wrong to do this and physically hand them back their shame using whatever prop is most appropriate.

There is also a fantastic technique called mirroring, where you watch the group play out a specific story in your life or act out a belief system you have. This can allow you to watch objectively an experience that you've perhaps been minimizing. This can help you understand the impact a situation may have had on you.

Some people don't like the idea of being on a stage and exposing themselves in front of a group of people they barely know. Yes, this can be stress-inducing, but it can also be very cathartic. With psychodrama, you can't just be an observer; you'll be actively encouraged to participate, so you'll need to go in with trust and an open mind.

Art Therapy

One long-standing belief that I've had about myself is that I am terrible at art. I have never been able to draw, and art lessons at school were terrifying for me. I would compare myself to everyone else and be hypercritical of anything I produced. So when I was encouraged to do art therapy, I felt a huge amount of dread. How was this therapy going to work for me if I was so bad at art?

Well, it turns out you don't have to be good at art to engage in this type of therapy. In fact, the final product doesn't really matter. Art therapy is more about the process of being creative, expressive and playful. It requires us to trust our intuition and not judge what comes up.[5]

Art therapy aims to raise our self-understanding, reduce stress, help us process our emotions and increase our sense of wellbeing.[6] It can also allow people to express experiences too traumatic or difficult to put into words.[7]

Ideally, art therapy should be conducted with a therapist. One exercise I found particularly useful is spontaneous expression, which aims to provide a window into our unconscious. You simply create an image of anything you want, using whatever materials you want. For example, you could use crayons to draw on a piece of paper, or you could create a collage. This can help you express any deep emotions, communicate how you feel and can then be discussed with your therapist.

YOUR CREATIVE JOURNAL

In *The Art Therapy Sourcebook*, Cathy A Malchiodi advises participants to keep a collection of spontaneous images.[8]

I want you to take some paper and a pen and draw whatever comes to your mind right now. If you want to use different materials, go ahead! Be creative. Create these images three or four times a week for a few weeks. Write a date on these and perhaps a few words about how it made you feel or how you would describe it.

Do you observe any patterns? What shapes, colours or themes emerge? What feelings do your drawings display?

Is there a part of the drawing you don't like? If so, make another drawing of that section, make it bigger and give it more detail. How does this new drawing make you feel?

Think back to our exercise in the last chapter, "Seeing the Feeling" (page 125) and sit with the feeling that your picture brings up. Use the feelings chart on page 124 to help you identify what you are experiencing. How does it feel to sit with this new feeling? What comes up? When you look back at your pictures, look at the date you drew them. What was going on in your life around that time? Do the pictures bring up memories of what you experienced at the time? Did drawing the picture help you process them? If you are seeing a therapist, it might be helpful to discuss your drawing and your feelings with them.

Music Therapy

Similar to art therapy, music therapy also aims to help participants express their emotions or their needs.[9] Again, you do not need to have a musical background or talent.

You can develop a therapeutic relationship with your therapist through playing together. This is often improvised, and the therapist will respond to what you need and what you want to create. This makes each session unique. Over time, a trust can develop which can allow the exploration of difficult emotions. A wide range of instruments or musical styles can be used, from percussion, to singing, to rap. If there is a song you just want to listen to or perform, that falls under the category of music therapy too![10] [11] Other examples of music therapy include analysing lyrics, songwriting and movement to music.

There is evidence that music therapy can have a positive impact on mood, stress, self-esteem and emotional expression.[12] [13]

Specifically for addiction, there is also evidence to suggest that music therapy can be used as an "add on" treatment to help with cravings and increase motivation for people with addictions to substances who are going through detox or short-term rehab. However, most of the studies were conducted in the same facility and the studies were very small.[14]

Journaling

I have given you a number of exercises throughout this book, all of which I recommend revisiting, but one of the most important therapeutic exercises of all is maintaining a regular journal.

I recommend journaling daily, but even doing it three to four times a week is great. The power of writing is so therapeutic as it validates our feelings and helps us process them. Studies have shown that journaling can help us accept, as opposed to judge, our mental experiences or the noise in our mind.[15]

Journaling isn't about writing something that needs to be perfect. In fact, staying away from structured writing is best a lot of the time, and stream-of-consciousness writing can be most helpful. It's ideal to keep an actual handwritten journal we can continually add to (it's also a time where we are not writing on a phone or laptop!). This allows us to chronologically review our notes from times we were struggling and remind ourselves how we got through it.

You're Not Alone

Despite being in recovery, I still get triggered by things, I still get anxious and I still respond to some things like a child. Thankfully, I have now developed a close group of friends with whom I feel comfortable asking for help. These aren't all new friends that I met in recovery. Some friends have come from simply adopting new hobbies and activities in my life.

I don't always find it easy to ask for help, but I now have much better awareness around what I need and when. I can ask myself whether a need I have is something I need from others or myself. There were many times in recovery when I felt rejected when asking for help. But the more this happened, the better I became at detaching from it and realizing it doesn't mean anything about me personally. Remember, people have their own struggles and may have to say no, even if they want to help!

You do not have to go through your addiction, your recovery or your life alone. Some of us might be lucky enough to have supportive friends and family, some of us may not. However, there is a lot of support out there, be it through your healthcare professional, the different 12-step fellowships, SMART Recovery or therapy.

I spoke to a friend of mine, A, who is a member of a 12-step fellowship. He has been in recovery for about the same time as me. We were talking about what has helped him keep his abstinence and enjoy life, not just get through it. He said that the best thing that has come out of his fellowship has been the friendship of others. Connection.

CHAPTER 10

ONE FOOT IN FRONT OF THE OTHER

Maintaining Our Recovery and Change

One thing I sometimes struggle with and see my clients struggle with too is the concept "Once an addict, always an addict". I don't mean that I struggle with being labelled an addict. I am proud of what I have been through and how I have turned my life around. However, what can be difficult is the notion that an addict can never be "cured". Instead, we must develop coping skills to help us let go of any urges or self-destructive behaviours as they arise.

We might have thoughts about using no matter how many years of recovery we have under our belts. That is totally normal and doesn't necessarily mean anything about our recovery. I still occasionally get thoughts about picking up a drink or trying drugs that I'd never tried before, but they don't have to impact me – they're just thoughts. It has now reached the point where I can honestly say that my addictive behaviours do not significantly impact my life.

Of course, therein lies a danger. During the early stages of recovery, while breaking habits and establishing new ones, we focus on self-care, mindfulness or therapy. We have a drive and a purpose to improve, and we may have a support group or sponsor to help us and keep us accountable. However, as the months and years go by, we may decide to set new goals for ourselves and build a life outside of recovery. We may have new stresses and priorities in our lives. As a result, we may start going to fewer meetings or stop our daily exercise routine. Perhaps we have a new job that doesn't give us as much time, or we have started a family. As time passes, we may feel guilt or shame that we get the occasional craving, or we may even question whether we were ever addicted in the first place.

We've previously talked about how to break patterns and change our habits. But as with all habits, making a lasting change is a challenge in itself. So, let's have a look at what can make us more likely to relapse and why that happens.

Relapse

Relapse is a common part of recovery, and it's vital to remember that you're not alone if this has been your experience. When I talk about relapse here, I don't mean just that single moment where we have used again, but also the subsequent return to the addictive cycle. Some therapists define a "lapse" as the initial re-use and then a "relapse" as the repeated use thereafter.[1]

Recovery is a long road, and there may well be bumps along the way. Due to the cravings that occur once we have put down our drug/behaviour of choice, sustaining abstinence can be quite tricky. According to the National Institute of Drug Abuse, the percentage of relapse in substance use disorders is between 40 and 60 per cent.[2] In one study, the percentage for relapse opioid addiction of a residential treatment centre in Ireland was as high as 91 per cent.[3] In this case, the highly addictive nature of opioids can make it much harder to abstain from them, even after a prolonged period of abstinence.

I imagine that relapse percentages are even higher when it comes to behavioural addictions such as gaming, shopping or phone addiction. We know that recovery from substance addiction requires abstinence and keeping away from the substance in day-to-day life as much as possible. But things like phones and shopping are around us all the time, so abstaining from addictive behaviours becomes more complicated.

Moments of relapse can feel like a backward step, as if all the previous hard work has been undone, but relapsing isn't necessarily a bad thing. The understanding of relapsing is usually one of doom and gloom, and although relapsing is painful, it is also a realistic part of recovery and something that is experienced by many.

It's important to remember that a relapse does not mean that the work before the relapse is invalidated, but rather, it is another step on the way to the hopeful goal of prolonged abstinence and recovery. People who relapse during recovery tend to be very critical of themselves.[4] But relapsing often turns out to be a teaching point.

A few of my clients have experienced relapse, but they go on to tell me that, in hindsight, they are grateful for these experiences as they have learned a lot about themselves and their recovery through the process. The main takeaway is that the relapse itself was coming over the horizon long before the metaphorical bottle touched their lips. Relapsing was cultivating itself in things like cutting corners and not prioritizing recovery. I personally know how easy it is not to turn up to an AA meeting because you just don't feel like it that day, but that is often how it starts.

So what does relapse look like? And what makes us more likely to relapse?

There is a common misconception that preventing relapse is just about rejecting a craving or urge when given the opportunity to use. However, relapse is more of a culmination of thoughts, feelings and stress that leads up to returning to the addictive behaviour. Although that moment of re-use is difficult to stop, if we can recognize the stages leading up to that use, then we can prevent that lapse from happening in the first place and create strategies to intervene.

We've already talked about how the brain changes because of substance misuse and some behavioural addictions. However, there has also been research as to why we, after a period of abstinence, might relapse and turn to those behaviours again.

In one study, rats were given levers to press to give themselves an addictive substance.[5] [6] Following this, the drug was no longer given on pressing the lever. The rats then learned that pressing the lever no longer gave them the drug. This is called "extinction" training. As a result, the rats eventually stopped pressing the lever as they learned that the drug was no longer available. Further research on these rats suggests that there are three main triggers to get them to relapse:

1. Re-exposure
2. A stressful event
3. Cues

Re-Exposure

After their extinction training, the rats were then given a single dose of the drug again. This was given via injection and not by pressing the lever. As a result of this, the rats started to press the lever again, indicating that re-exposure to the substance made them more likely to restart their addictive behaviour.

A Stressful Event

You may have heard of someone turning back to a substance or to an addictive behaviour after a period of trauma. For example, someone experiences a relapse from their gambling addiction as a result of a relationship breakdown, or they turn back to an addictive substance after they suffer a bereavement. Studies assessing alcohol relapse indicate that highly stressful events can increase the chance of relapse. There is also some evidence that stress and low mood can be associated with increased cravings for alcohol.[7]

In a further study on our rats who had previously been exposed to a substance, "addicted" and then subsequently abstinent, the rats were given an acute stress, this time an electric shock to their feet. The stress of this shock caused them to seek out the drug again and start pressing the lever. This occurred across a wide range of substances including heroin, cocaine, nicotine and alcohol.

Cues

In a similar study, our rats were this time exposed to alcohol upon pressing the lever and at the same time given two stimuli when the alcohol came: smell and light. Following extinction training, the rats started to press the lever again when they were exposed to the light and the smell, even five months after they last received the alcohol.[8] [9]

You may remember Pavlov's study of dogs. During his research, Pavlov fed his dogs food after ringing a bell. Eventually the dogs associated the bell – the cue – with food and started salivating just on hearing the bell ring. They learned that the bell meant food was coming.

For me, packing for a holiday became a cue associated with restricting my food. I would always use going away as an excuse to eat less as I was going to be in a bikini, which made me feel even more self-conscious than usual. Therefore, the process of packing would be a cue for me to start obsessing about my weight.

High-Risk Situations

So now we know that re-exposure, stressful events and associated cues can all make us go back into the addictive cycle in a laboratory setting. But how might this look in practice? In their relapse prevention model, G Alan Marlatt and Judith R Gordon suggested that there are "high-risk" situations which can act as a trigger for alcoholics to use after a period of abstinence.[10]

"High-risk" situations were later categorized to include:

1 **Negative emotional states:** Such as feeling angry or depressed.
2 **Interpersonal situations:** For example, having an argument with somebody.
3 **Social pressure:** This can be either direct (someone is inviting you out for drinks) or indirect (such as being at a party where everyone is drinking).
4 **Positive emotional states:** For example, during a time of celebration. This can also include exposure to alcohol-related cues such as going to a restaurant to celebrate a promotion or meeting a friend at a shopping centre for their birthday.[11]

Three Stages of Relapse

With that in mind, let's talk about how a relapse might develop and what the different stages may look like. As I mentioned, relapse is often a gradual process and often starts weeks or months before the person repeats the addictive behaviour. This means that we may have an opportunity to recognize these patterns early, and this will allow us to apply our coping strategies before we fall back into the addictive cycle.

There are various models of relapse, but I like to use the model devised by Dr Steven Melemis, addiction specialist and author, with my clients. He defines three stages of relapse:[12]

1 Emotional relapse
2 Mental relapse
3 Physical relapse

Emotional Relapse

This is the earliest stage and may occur gradually. It often happens during a period of poor emotional and physical self-care. At this point we do not have any conscious plans to start using; we remember what we were like during the addictive cycle, and we don't want to go back there.

However, we might be going through a difficult period in our lives, or we might be more stressed, anxious or irritable. This ties in with the "negative emotional state" of Marlatt and Gordon's model. Our sleep might be interrupted, or we haven't had the time to cook recently and our diet has worsened. As a result, we might not have the energy or the time to attend our support groups.

We may not ask for help from our support network, keeping our emotions inside and isolating ourselves. We might concentrate on other people's struggles and emotions or be more conscious about how other people's actions impact us.

This is a situation that can happen to any of us at any time in our lives. Unfortunately, being tired, anxious, irritable or low in mood can make us more susceptible to thoughts of engaging in our addictive behaviour and may prompt us to think of ways outside ourselves to make us feel good again. Therefore, if we stay in this place for a while, then we may slip into the next stage of relapse.

Mental Relapse

As we stay in this emotional relapse, the thoughts and desires to engage in our addictive behaviour increase. There is still a part of us that does not want to relapse. However, we start to think more and more about our use and the people or cues involved, and we start to have more euphoric recall. Our cravings therefore increase, and we think about situations where it would be acceptable to use. This is called bargaining.

Bargaining can be quite loud. It can be like a washing machine of thoughts and negotiation within ourselves as we wrestle with our own conscience. It is a way we can create excuses for ourselves and cut corners. This, of course, can lead to relapse. For example, saying to ourselves, "I will only drink at my friend's wedding, but then stop again" or "I can smoke weed because weed was never my drug of choice" or "I am only allowed to go shopping during the sales". In this state, we are more susceptible to those high-risk situations for relapse.

Physical Relapse

This, of course, is the stage where we engage in the addictive behaviour or take the addictive substance again. This usually occurs when we think we will get away with it and no one will find out. However, as we have seen with our rats, once we have lapsed, we are then more likely to restart our continued use and fall back into the addictive cycle.

Let's look at an example of these stages of relapse. I have a client who suffered from love and sex addiction. She wanted to sustain her abstinence for a prolonged period of time, but she struggled due to the intense loneliness she felt when being on her own. Her abstinence consisted of not messaging any ex-partners, and if they texted her, she would create space and reach out to close friends or a sponsor.

After about three or four months of abstinence, she started feeling better and stronger in herself and continued to be vigilant about reaching out to others and keeping honest about how she was feeling. However, after about six months, she had some stress at work and wasn't sleeping as well. *A potential sign of emotional relapse.* She noticed the loneliness creep back in. She didn't reach out to her support group as she felt she couldn't keep boring people about it. *Isolating herself.* She kept her feelings to herself and convinced herself that she didn't need anyone else's help. *Keeping her emotions inside.* She knew the plan, and if her ex messaged her, of course she wouldn't reply. It had been six months!

You may be able to recognize the signs of a potential emotional relapse here. After a month or two, she felt the loneliness and anxiety build and become less bearable. At this point, she began to have dreams about her ex and fantasies of getting back in touch. *Increased cravings: a potential sign of a mental relapse.* Surely, they were soul mates and enough time had passed that they could be friends. She told me that she thought she could at least text her ex on his birthday. *Bargaining.* This prompted her one day to write a sporadic text message to the best friend of her ex – just to find out how he was doing. *Seeking associated people or cues.* This only triggered more feelings and impulses around her love addiction, and later that week she lapsed. She got back in touch with her ex. Following this lapse, she unfortunately relapsed into the toxic cycle she had been in before.

Working through this together in therapy in a non-judgemental manner enabled my client to notice that the relapse had started at a time when she thought she was still in total control. She could see that, as time passed, she became a little more complacent and a little more in denial about the fact that she had previously felt so much pain while stuck in her addictive cycle.

Causes of Relapse

In my experience, personally and professionally, some of the biggest causes of relapse are denial that you were ever an addict in the first place, complacency and the relationships we engage in (mainly the romantic type).

Denial Revisited

We've talked extensively about denial already, but it's worth repeating that if you don't really think you're an addict in the first place, this makes it very hard for recovery to be a priority in your life. The door will always be slightly ajar for the moments you want to fall back on the narrative of "Well, I don't think I was *really* an addict anyway."

Complacency

Complacency can take many forms. The most common example is saying something like, "Ah well, I've been sober for two years, it's my daughter's wedding, half a glass of champagne won't hurt. I can always come back from this." We think that if we have done a few years sober it will be easy to jump back on the recovery bandwagon – but this is usually not the case. We forget how powerful and alluring the addictive cycle is.

There have definitely been times over the years that I have been close to relapse. Mainly because I forget that I am an addict or have struggled to acknowledge that I am an addict, but also because recovery is not the priority in my life anymore. The first two years of my recovery felt the safest because recovery was the most important thing in my life (it had to be). Therefore I had a lot of support around me, which acted as a deterrent against relapse. It was after I had a few years under my belt that I became a bit complacent. Even today I have to remind myself that I cannot afford to become sloppy.

Relationships

Francis Lickerish explained that, in his experience, romantic relationships are the second-biggest cause of relapse, after complacency. Why? Well, these relationships bring out trauma patterns in people. These are the ones that trigger a deep pain – abandonment, shame, the need to be perfect. They can cause such intense feelings that relapse can become almost inevitable sometimes.[13] I found this to be true when I started dating a little bit prematurely – I was one year clean but certainly not at the stage where I could handle rejection. I had to take a step back and put off dating for another few years. This wasn't easy as I had been so used to being validated through my love life, but I knew it was essential if I wanted to maintain my recovery.

When I finally did come around to dating a few years later, it really tested me. I remember the bargaining going on in my head when I arrived at the bar one night for a date. I told myself there was no harm in just having one drink. I didn't want my date to ask why I wasn't drinking as I was still ashamed of my addiction. I went to the bar to order a gin and tonic. I usually drank wine, and this was a different drink, so surely that was okay. Luckily, at that moment I looked at my phone and had a text from a friend in recovery. He was wishing me luck on my date. Thankfully, that was enough to prompt me to make a different choice.

I can say from experience that if someone doesn't want to date you because you don't drink, that says a lot more about them than it does about you. You are much more likely to find the right person for you if you're yourself!

Preventing Relapse

So, how do we prevent ourselves from falling into a relapse? What coping strategies can we use to help us if we find ourselves wanting to repeat our addictive behaviour? These are what have really worked for me:

1 **Avoiding cues** or at least being aware of cues and associated behaviours which might tempt us into using.
2 **Being honest** with ourselves and with others.

3 **Asking for help** from friends, family, support groups and therapy.
4 **Maintaining self-care** by sticking with our routines, sleep, exercise and journaling.

Avoiding Cues

In 12-step fellowships, there is a popular phrase that says that to maintain and sustain our recovery, we should change or be aware of "people, places and things". Essentially, we need to try to avoid people, places and things that we associate with our past substance use or addictive behaviour. This is based on the associated cues we have discussed previously and on the experiments on our rats. This phrase was a powerful reminder whenever I wanted to go back into an environment that had previously been dangerous for me.

When working with clients who are trying to maintain their recovery, we look at these factors and often work on letting go of the environments that they once enjoyed. They don't find festivals fun without drugs, or they can't hang out with their group of friends who they smoked weed with. There is sometimes a sense of loss with this, and that is absolutely normal. The reality is that the urges to go back to those things that were once so familiar might never leave. And that's okay. We just need to learn that those people, places or things might not be what is right for our future selves. That doesn't mean we won't still grieve it for years to come. But were we really happy at that point in our lives anyway?

Some clients have said to me that they think avoiding risky situations is actually a sign of weakness. Just because they aren't using or drinking, surely that doesn't mean they have to stay away from their former environment; they just need to "be strong" or "suck it up". This is certainly not kind, and I challenge the reason for them wanting to put themselves in that situation. What are they trying to prove, and who are they trying to prove it to?

It's also worth mentioning that if people ask why you don't drink, why you don't play games anymore or why you don't want to place a bet, you don't owe them an explanation. Simply saying "I don't feel like it tonight" is a good enough reason!

Being Honest

We know from our denial chapter that being an addict involves deceiving ourselves and other people, and that being honest is one of the key steps of recovery. We may fear that, even after years of recovery, being honest with our emotions and our struggles might bore or appal others. However, I think you may find that it brings you closer to others. We talked about connection being the antithesis of addiction. Being honest with ourselves and others, and allowing others to see and understand our insecurities, can solidify friendships and help us build these connections.[14]

If your story is one where relapse features, getting honest about that will be the thing that saves you from another relapse. We don't want to give the shame another reason to keep us going back into old patterns – remember, shame dies on exposure! Being honest with ourselves is also a part of this. Remember how strong denial can be at times – it isn't harmful to ask if you're being honest with yourself.

Honesty remains a key part of maintaining recovery, and if we find ourselves keeping secrets again, this can be a sign of relapse. I have found that voicing whatever thought comes into my head has saved me from acting recklessly. I really understand now that my thoughts are *not* reality.

It's especially important to be honest with ourselves during stressful events or when we catch ourselves bargaining. Sometimes these things go hand in hand. For example, stressful events for me were always around Christmas and New Year. This was a time of year I dreaded because the emphasis was always on drinking, food and the "fun" that came with both those things. This time was stressful for me for family reasons too, so I always found myself bargaining about how maybe those were the times I could give myself a "treat" – it was the holidays after all.

Usually, if we find ourselves bargaining, it means we should probably look at the situation with complete honesty. We are always capable of manipulating our circumstances and making something fit our narrative, but we will always be short-changing ourselves if we do.

When you have the urge to go back to old patterns, try creating space between yourself and the stressful event. When you get the thought that you will be okay to just have one drink, to just download Instagram for a quick look or to just place one bet, wait. Pause. Take an hour or two and consider honestly what consequences might occur. The stressful event might be very overwhelming, but is it worth drinking over? Is it worth engaging in old self-destructive patterns?

Asking for Help

Asking for help when we need it is so important. This of course includes emotional support, but it also extends beyond that. Asking someone for support to share some of the day-to-day load and give us some extra room to breathe can be essential in helping keep our recovery afloat.

I have a very good friend in recovery who has always struggled to ask for help. Once we were chatting, and I asked if she needed anything at that moment in time that she felt she couldn't ask for. She told me that what she really needed was help with watering her plants while she was away. This might seem like a simple task. However, asking someone this gave her a lot of anxiety as she didn't want to be a burden on anybody else. Once she started asking for this from those around her, she realized that other things she needed help with, like emotional support, became much easier to ask for as a result.

Asking for help doesn't have to be limited to friends and family. As I mentioned last chapter, therapy can be a great help to get you started on the road to recovery, and it can continue to support recovery by working with any unresolved trauma that might lead to relapse. We have talked extensively about how addictive behaviours can bring us out of ourselves and can be a distraction from what we feel inside. So it makes sense that using therapy to address feelings we have been avoiding will be beneficial. If we no longer feel uncomfortable within ourselves, or stressed, or shameful, then we might not need to engage in our addictive behaviour.

Reaching out for help from support groups can also allow us to remain vigilant around how relapse can rear its head, remind us how that devil on our shoulder sounds and protect us from complacency.

Making sure we have all the help we need in whatever form we choose will be vital during the journey of recovery and change.

Maintaining Self-Care

I for one know that if I don't take care of myself on the most basic level (for example, food, sleep, water, movement, etc.), then all the other stuff can easily fall apart.

Self-care can look different from person to person, and we have talked about developing routines as well as keeping healthy habits in our previous chapters. One additional tip that I have found very helpful over the years is considering the acronym HALT. This stands for Hungry, Angry, Lonely, Tired. When you feel uncomfortable feelings or are at the end of your tether, reminding yourself of this acronym can be useful to prevent destructive behaviour.

If you are either hungry, angry, lonely or tired, first think of how you can meet this need before turning to a self-destructive behaviour. Being hungry, angry, lonely or tired is uncomfortable, and we will no doubt want to change that feeling – this can lead to cravings. Meeting these needs – be it by satiating our hunger, having a nap, reaching out to a friend or constructively channelling our anger – can prevent us from doing anything we might later regret.

This not only helps encourage space between us and our cravings, it also helps us realize our needs at times we might be feeling uncomfortable or vulnerable. A lot of us were never taught to ask ourselves what we need, and this can be a good exercise in training our minds to make that a priority. This can prevent us from looking outside of ourselves to feel soothed.

Let's look at feeling tired a bit more. It took me years to come to terms with the fact that rest was one of the most important things in maintaining my recovery. I found it so hard to sit still – I really believed that the more I busied myself, the more it would help my mind rest. However, I know now that I was keeping myself busy to avoid those pesky thoughts and feelings.

My key to prioritizing rest is scheduling it into the week. If it is in my schedule, then I am much more likely to take that time for myself, even if it feels uncomfortable. When I find myself in periods of my life where I feel especially overwhelmed or stressed, I must make sure that I take time out even more regularly. I am someone who likes to tick things off a list; it gives me a sense of control. But life doesn't always work like this. Sometimes it can feel like too much because I can't get everything done in one day.

So, during these times I aim for five minutes of stillness, three times a day. I know that might seem like a lot, but fifteen minutes is not a long time in the grand scheme of things, and it can have a very powerful effect. These five-minute bursts can look however you like. It can be five minutes of breathing, journaling or, my favourite, sitting on the floor with my legs crossed and without expectation – just trying to sit still. As I mentioned before, a lot of the time, relapse starts way before picking up a substance or behaviour, so taking time to rest will help prevent these impulsive moments.

DREAMING BIG

Finally it's time for my favourite exercise – creating a vision board. This exercise ties in with what we have been talking about this chapter – maintaining the life that we want for ourselves.

A while back, my therapist told me to create a vision board, and I found myself procrastinating as I thought anything creative was not for me. How wrong I was! This exercise is really inspiring, fun and healing on many levels. This is something that you can take your time with and can keep returning to over the next few weeks.

It's best to get a big piece of paper or a foam board that you can stick things onto.

Then I want you to think about what you want for your life. What are the things you have always wanted but never dared to go for? With this in mind, start looking through old magazines or on the internet. When you see pictures that resonate with you, simply cut them out or print them and stick them on your board.

You can get as creative as you like, especially if you like to draw – perhaps using coloured pens or paints. There is no right or wrong – what you want for your life is entirely up to you. It could be a car that you have always dreamed of, or a pet that you have always wanted in your life. The options are limitless.

This is a special project where you are fully with yourself, perhaps giving yourself permission for the first time to really ask yourself what you want. It will help you gain clarity about where you want to be in the future and help you solidify long-term goals.

You can keep adding to your board over time, or you can create new ones when you feel it's necessary.

It's very important to place your vision board somewhere where you'll see it often. I myself have a vision board that I made six years ago next to my bed, and as my life has evolved over the years, it has been interesting to see what has come to fruition and what has ended up being different. It's time for me to start my next one too!

The Long and Winding Road

Many of you reading this may not be recovering addicts, and so this concept of relapsing might be foreign. The *Oxford English Dictionary* defines relapse as "A deterioration in someone's state of health after a temporary improvement".[15] Maybe there have been moments in your life when you have felt like you have deteriorated after a period of improvement. When you have had a period of not scrolling first thing in the morning, but then you find yourself back to doing it daily. Or when you have time away from online shopping, but then without realizing it you have spent your monthly wages on clothes you don't need. Perhaps you had a period of time without binging on sugar, but then you don't want to say no to your friend's birthday cake and you find yourself binging for days afterwards.

Perhaps we could call these experiences forms of relapsing, or we could just see them as opportunities for learning. What has our experience taught us? What can we put in place so this doesn't happen next time? Can we notice a pattern? Journaling can help you recognize any such patterns.

Recovery is a lifelong journey. That may sound daunting, but it is something I have learned to live with and am at peace with. It's made me more content and in harmony with myself and with life than I ever believed possible. It's created new relationships with people I cherish and shaped old relationships into ones which are more stable, mutual and fulfilling. Not only this, but it's allowed me to have a better relationship with myself. Is it worth the price of intermittent cravings, FOMO (fear of missing out) and being vulnerable with people around me? Absolutely.

I say this not to brag, but to tell you it is worth it and it can be done. Recovery will have bumps in the road – we might lapse, relapse or face challenges and struggles. But by avoiding cues, continuing to be honest, asking for help, focusing on rest and self-care, and self-reflecting and journaling, we can remain vigilant of any complacency, denial and emotional relapse before it's too late.

Finally, my advice is to be gentle. Listen to your body, don't judge your emotions, and lean on your friends and support groups. Try not to shut out the warning signs or the advice of others. Be open and honest, and you'll get to wherever you want to be. Start slow, but don't be afraid to dream big!

CONCLUSION

Like the rings within the trunk of a tree, what we have been through in our lives stays within us. That is inescapable. Some of these rings will remember happy, nourishing times, others will be scars of past traumas or the negative self-beliefs we harbour within us. It is understandable that we want to distract ourselves from doubts, bad memories or the everyday stresses we encounter. Indeed, having some leisure time or participating in a hobby is a positive thing.

However, fast-hitting, short-lived, addictive substances and behaviours short-circuit our reward pathways with intense hits of dopamine. They may make us feel good or numb us from our troubles in the moment, but they come at a cost. Our brains begin to get used to these hits and begin to build a tolerance, making it harder and harder to reach that same level of high. Our addictive behaviours may put us in debt, alienate our friends or family, damage our physical and mental health, prevent us from achieving our goals or interrupt our careers. All the while, the reasons that we use in the first place remain unchecked.

Our brains and our defence mechanisms give us the impression that these behaviours are positive or necessary. As a result, it can be difficult to see the addictive cycles we find ourselves in.

Through my lived experience, my training, my professional practice, my peer support and my literature review, I want you to take away the following recommendations which turned my life around:

1. Don't Be Afraid to Feel

As humans, we tend to want to only feel good feelings and avoid the bad. However, those bad feelings tell us what we need and give us clues on what we need to work on. Here's my top two tips on how to focus in on your feelings:

- Practice mindfulness or meditation – a minimum of five minutes, three times a day is ideal!
- Find time when you are not distracted, when you can be grounded in the here and now. This could be sitting quietly at home, cooking or going for a walk. Notice the feelings that come and go. Try not to judge them.
- Journal: Actively write down your thoughts and feelings and reflect on them. Try not to judge these either!

2. Break the Patterns

Our brains have learned these habits, and so can unlearn them too. Working on breaking unhealthy habits and creating new, fulfilling ones can help us reforge positive feedback loops between what we do and how we feel. Here's my top tips on breaking the patterns:

- Map your addictive behaviours. Objectively analysing your use may help chip away at your denial or inspire you to act. Consider the following:
    - When I use: Understand the circumstances of your use.
    - Who I use with: Think about who influences your use and how you might address this with them.
    - The highs: Listing the benefits of your behaviour can help you identify why you feel you need to use.
    - The lows: Understanding the negative consequences of your addictive behaviours is critical to recovery.

- Plan for the following:
  - How will you replace the benefits of your addictive behaviour? Think about kinder or healthier ways as alternatives to those perceived benefits.
  - How will you avoid associated cues? Consider who and where you use and think of ways to avoid these triggers.
  - Where will you receive support? Contemplate receiving support from friends, family, peer support groups or professional therapists.

- ACT:
  - **A**bstinence: A controlled, safe abstinence helps our brains rebalance and break the addictive cycle.
  - **B**e mindful of cravings: Distract yourself by going for a walk or calling a friend, or simply be mindful that the feelings will eventually pass.
  - **C**reate new, healthy habits: Consider starting small, simple and at a regular time or place. Ask a friend to come with you and don't forget to reward yourself.

3. Consider Therapy

Not everybody will need therapy to stop addictive behaviours. But I still recommend therapy to everyone and anyone, addicted or not! It is a great way to dissect the feelings that come up when we sit with ourselves. It helps chip away at any denial we might have and it gives us the opportunity to understand and explore ourselves and our belief systems and process any shame we may be carrying.

4. Maintain Your Recovery

Remember that the seeds of relapse are often sown before the act itself. You can do this by:

- Continuing to be honest and open to yourself and your support circle.
- Being wary of people, places and things. Avoid potential triggers of your past use.
- Prioritizing your self-care. Think about Hungry, Angry, Lonely, Tired (HALT). Try to meet any of these needs before thinking about using or acting self-destructively.

Final Thoughts

I hope this book brings about lasting change for you. How significant that change will be is determined by the addictive behaviour you practice, your individual circumstances and how much effort you put into the change. Even if it just means putting down your phone for an extra hour a day, that is a victory!

Ultimately, I think addiction is about running from our own truth. The truth about who we are, where we come from and how we feel – not just how we feel about ourselves, but the feelings we experience from day to day. Writing this book has stirred up emotions in me, feelings I thought I had dealt with and questions about who I am as a therapist or – dare I say it – author. I don't think the journey of self-discovery ever really ends. But it's a journey I'm so grateful to be on. No one is perfect. There will be bumps in the road, and there may be times when you just want to give up, but you can get there too, one step at a time.

APPENDIX

A Letter From My Mother

* Some names have been changed for privacy

Darling Talitha,

Few babies will have been more wanted, prayed for and expected than you were, and your birth was a miracle, as far as I was concerned. And if I was only ever going to have one baby, I wanted it to be a little girl ... and there you were! All pink and smooth and round and cuddly.

This little baby grew into an inquisitive, sunny, active toddler and then little girl. Always busy. Always chatty. You had a presence and a personality that drew people to you, and I loved your company.

You started to change around the age of 10 or 11, imperceptibly became obsessive about your friendships and in some of your behaviour. I did not notice at first and then I did not understand. I did not know what to do about it.

You went to school and I stopped seeing you. You were away, and when you were at home you adapted your behaviour so that it would hide whatever was going on. Then I noticed that you started to eliminate certain foods. Then you became secretive, lied, told me what you thought I wanted to hear. You were 15.

I wanted to believe you, but watching you change out of your sport clothes one day shocked me. It was a jolt to me. I needed to do something to rescue you. I was your mummy and I needed to care for you. Make you better.

That was the start of a long, long spiral of despair, anger, frustration, helplessness, bewilderment, rage, visceral fear. Sleepless nights. Years of it. Never-ending darkness. At times it felt like my heart was being ripped out and trampled on. And I felt so lonely in trying to deal with it. I felt like a bad mummy.

I have suppressed a lot of the significant details or traumatic events linked to your eating disorder, and so I find it very difficult to recall them. The most recent and traumatic one was on your birthday, in Cap Benat. You had invited 20 friends over to the house and had asked for a big paella. It was fabulous, and everybody was really excited about it.

Then, 30 minutes before your guests were about to arrive, you went to the kitchen, got half a beetroot from the fridge, put it on your plate and sat at the dining table. You were having your dinner (if you could call it that) before your party started and before your guests arrived. It was surreal and painful to watch. I tried very hard to pretend it wasn't happening so I could suppress the urge to tell you to stop, to slap you back into reality, to make you acknowledge how absurd this was.

M and T both noticed and looked at me with an air of desperation, shock and disbelief at the gravity of the situation. It was torture, and I still find it painful to recall. I felt a failure for not being able to stop it. I don't want to recall any other similar moments.

For a brief moment, when you had been sober and clean for a few months, and before your eating disorder kicked in, I found you again. My fabulous, luminous, engaging, selfless, funny and charismatic girl. The one I recognized and enjoyed chatting to and spending time with and sharing stuff with. You were wise and kind. The one I was proud of introducing to my friends and having around. The one that understood me, that had shared the break up of our traditional family unit into something different, but something that was supportive and cosy.

But slowly the Monster grew in you. You looked like Puce, but you did not behave like Puce. It was so confusing. The Monster was breathtakingly self-obsessed, narcissistic. The Monster lived for selfies and how many likes it got on Instagram.

The Monster lived for drama.

But worse than all that, the Monster lied and manipulated. The Monster knew to go and talk to F, for example, and tell her that the reason it did not eat was because its mummy did not love it. It knew that F would be very upset by this and would talk to her mummy who would then talk to me and accuse me of being a bad mother. This makes me cry.

The drama surrounding the Monster became too toxic for me to bear. It was dragging me down into a dark place. It was damaging my relationships with other people I love: Maxie, T, my girlfriends. I had to sever any contact with the Monster in order to save my healthy relationships, my sanity, to stop the endless sleepless nights of worry, the torture of watching the Monster that was Puce slowly dying.

The other thing that happened was that the thinner you became, the more repulsed I became by your body. I became unable to touch, hug or cuddle you. Even planting a kiss on your cheek revolted me. Touching you brought home the message even more forcefully that you were wasting away and dying. I decided that it was easier to pretend that Puce, my girl, my child, had died and therefore I had to turn the page and get on with my life without her.

This is where I stand today: I am mourning.

But I am also free: I no longer have to live with the Monster. I am no longer surrounded by drama. I can laugh. I can relax. I no longer have to worry about going to restaurants, buying food, keeping the right stuff in the fridge, stocking up on oat cakes or beetroot. I no longer have to worry about upsetting the Monster, gauging its mood, making sure it is okay. I am no longer dragged down if the Monster is having a bad day. I am no longer anxious and that feels so, so good. I am allowed to enjoy life and I no longer have to feel shame or failure.

I have been asked if I can recall any significant events in your life that have impacted you.

As you know, you are a much-desired IVF baby. When I finally became pregnant with you, after seven failed attempts, I spent my pregnancy worrying that I might lose you. Did my anxiousness drive up my cortisol levels to the extent that you were born with a higher-than-normal level of cortisol? Is this partly responsible for your addictions? Who knows?

When you were 8, 9, 10 years old, you were obsessed with the notion that Daddy and I might divorce. Every night before putting you to bed you had to go through an obsessive routine involving lining up all your soft toys and making sure no burglars could come in through your window (on the fourth floor), and then you would make me promise that Daddy and I would not divorce. And I made that promise. Because at that time, I had no idea that this was even on the cards. As far as I was concerned, I was in a stable marriage. Only when you were 11 or 12 did your worst nightmare come true.

Apart from that you have grown up with two parents (although divorced) and a brother who love you. Your extended family of aunts, uncles and grandparents all love you. You have had a world-class education and every material comfort possible.

Only you know how this may have impacted your life.

Your mummy who loves you.

FURTHER RESOURCES

If you are seeking therapeutic help, you may find these resources helpful:

UK Resources

Therapy

Mind therapists work on a pay-what-you-can basis: www.mind.org.uk/information-support/drugs-and-treatments/talking-therapy-and-counselling/how-to-find-a-therapist/

This counselling directory can help you search for different types of therapy, online or in person and at different price points: www.counselling-directory.org.uk

Addiction-Specific Anonymous Groups

Alcoholics Anonymous: www.alcoholics-anonymous.org.uk
Narcotics Anonymous: www.ukna.org
Sex & Love Addicts Anonymous: www.slaauk.org
Codependent Anonymous: www.codauk.org
Overeaters Anonymous: www.oagb.org.u
Gamblers Anonymous: www.gamblersanonymous.org.uk

Extra Resources

AlAnon UK: www.al-anonuk.org.uk
SMART Recovery: www.smartrecovery.org.uk

The two treatment centres I visited

Start2Stop: www.start2stop.co.uk
Montrose Treatment Centre: www.montrosemanor.co.za

US Resources

Therapy

The American Psychological Association provides a psychologist locator: www.locator.apa.org
The National Register of Health Service Psychologists provides the same: www.findapsychologist.org

Addiction-Specific Anonymous Groups

Alcoholic Anonymous: www.aa.org
Narcotics Anonymous: www.na.org
Sex and Love Addicts Anonymous: www.slaafws.org
Codependent Anonymous: www.coda.org
Overeaters Anonymous: www.oa.org
Gamblers Anonymous: www.gamblersanonymous.org
Anorexic & Bulimic Anonymous: www.aba12steps.org

Extra Resources

AlAnon US: www.al-anon.org
SMART Recovery: www.smartrecovery.org

ENDNOTES

What Is Addiction?

1 Brand, Gerard. "Paul Merson: My message to gambling addicts." Sky Sports, n.d. www.skysports.com/football/story-telling/15205/12499030/paul-merson-my-message-to-gambling-addicts

2 Martin, E A, and Tanya A McFerran. *A Dictionary of Nursing*. Oxford: Oxford University Press, 2008

3 "Is Addiction Really a Disease?" IU Health, 13 July 2023. iuhealth.org/thrive/is-addiction-really-a-disease

4 Crocq, Marc-Antoine. "Historical and Cultural Aspects of Man's Relationship with Addictive Drugs." *Dialogues in Clinical Neuroscience* 9, no. 4 (2007): 355–61. doi.org/10.31887/dcns.2007.9.4/macrocq

5 "Is A.A. for You?" Alcoholics Anonymous, 2023. www.aa.org/self-assessment

6 Genetics and Epigenetics of Addiction DrugFacts, August 2019. www.nida.nih.gov/publications/drugfacts/genetics-epigenetics-addiction

7 Liu, Mengzhen, Yu Jiang, Robbee Wedow, Yue Li, David M Brazel, Fang Chen, Gargi Datta, et al. "Association Studies of up to 1.2 Million Individuals Yield New Insights into the Genetic Etiology of Tobacco and Alcohol Use." *Nature Genetics* 51, no. 2 (2019): 237–44. doi.org/10.1038/s41588-018-0307-5

8 Duffy, V, J Peterson and L Bartoshuk. "Associations between Taste Genetics, Oral Sensation and Alcohol Intake." *Physiology & Behavior* 82, no. 2–3 (2004): 435–45. doi.org/10.1016/j.physbeh.2004.04.060

9 Edenberg, Howard J, and Tatiana Foroud. "Genetics and Alcoholism." *Nature Reviews Gastroenterology & Hepatology* 10, no. 8 (2013): 487–94. doi.org/10.1038/nrgastro.2013.86

10 Blum, Kenneth, David Baron, Lisa Lott, Jessica V Ponce, David Siwicki, Brent Boyett, Bruce Steinberg, et al. "In Search of Reward Deficiency Syndrome (RDS)-Free Controls: The 'Holy Grail' in Genetic Addiction Risk Testing." *Current Psychopharmacology* 9, no. 1 (2020): 7–21. doi.org/10.2174/2211556008666191111103152

11 Filbey, Francesca M. "Is Addiction a Reward Deficiency Syndrome?" Essay. In *The Neuroscience of Addiction* (Cambridge, Cambridge University Press, 2019), 55–55

12 Kótyuk, Eszter, Marc N Potenza, Kenneth Blum and Zsolt Demetrovics. "The Reward Deficiency Syndrome and Links with Addictive and Related Behaviors." *Handbook of Substance Misuse and Addictions*, 2022, 59–74. doi.org/10.1007/978-3-030-92392-1_3

13 Edenberg, Howard J. "The Genetics of Alcohol Metabolism: Role of Alcohol Dehydrogenase and Aldehyde Dehydrogenase Variants." *Alcohol Research & Health* 30, no. 1 (2007): 5–13

14 Lee, Jack J. "Alcohol, 'asian Glow' Mutation May Contribute to Alzheimer's Disease, Study Finds." News Center, 11 December 2019. www.med.stanford.edu/news/all-news/2019/12/alcohol-asian-glow-mutation-may-contribute-to-alzheimers.html

15 Felitti, Vincent J, Robert F Anda, Dale Nordenberg, David F Williamson, Alison M Spitz, Valerie Edwards, Mary P Koss and James S Marks. "Relationship of Childhood Abuse and Household Dysfunction to Many of the Leading Causes of Death in Adults." *American Journal of Preventive Medicine* 14, no. 4 (1998): 245–58. doi.org/10.1016/s0749-3797(98)00017-8

16 Svanberg, Jenny. "The Impact of Early Life Adversity." Essay. In *The Psychology of Addiction* (London; New York: Routledge, Taylor et Francis Group, 2018), 55–56

The Many Things We Can Be Addicted To

1 Lembke, Anna. *Dopamine Nation: Finding Balance in the Age of Indulgence*. London: Headline Publishing Group, 2023

2 Rideout, Victoria J, Ulla G Foehr and Donald F Roberts. "Media in the Lives of 8- to 18-Year-Olds." Menlo Park, California: Kaiser Family Foundation, 2010

3 "ICD-11 for Mortality and Morbidity Statistics." World Health Organization, January 2023. http://id.who.int/icd/entity/338347362

4 Zendle, David, Rachel Meyer, Paul Cairns, Stuart Waters and Nick Ballou. "The Prevalence of Loot Boxes in Mobile and Desktop Games." *Addiction* 115, no. 9 (2020): 1768–72. doi.org/10.1111/add.14973

5 Clarkson, Adam. "Coronavirus: The Gamers Spending Thousands on Loot Boxes." BBC News, 13 November 2020. www.bbc.co.uk/news/uk-england-54906393

6 Sherer, James. "Internet Gaming." Psychiatry.org, January 2023. www.psychiatry.org/patients-families/internet-gaming

7 Mandriota, Morgan. "Gaming Disorder: Symptoms, Causes, and Treatments." Psych Central, 5 January 2022. www.psychcentral.com/addictions/gaming-disorder

8 Mohammad, Shabina, Raghad A Jan and Saba L Alsaedi. "Symptoms, Mechanisms, and Treatments of Video Game Addiction." *Cureus*, 2023. doi.org/10.7759/cureus.36957

9 Rajesh, Thipparapu, and Dr B Rangaiah. "Facebook Addiction and Personality." *Heliyon* 6, no. 1 (2020). doi.org/10.1016/j.heliyon.2020.e03184

10 Molino, Monica, Liliya Scafuri Kovalchuk, Chiara Ghislieri and Paola Spagnoli. "Work Addiction among Employees and Self-Employed Workers: An Investigation Based on the Italian Version of the Bergen Work Addiction Scale." *Europe's Journal of Psychology* 18, no. 3 (2022): 279–92. doi.org/10.5964/ejop.2607

11 Andreassen, Cecilie Schou, Mark D Griffiths, Jørn Hetland and Ståle Pallesen. "Development of a Work Addiction Scale." *Scandinavian Journal of Psychology* 53, no. 3 (2012): 265–72. doi.org/10.1111/j.1467-9450.2012.00947.x

12 "Gambling-Related Harms Evidence Review: Summary." Public Health England, 11 January 2023. www.gov.uk/government/publications/gambling-related-harms-evidence-review/gambling-related-harms-evidence-review-summary--2

13 "Tony Blair's Bet on Gambling Britain Has Spiralled Out of Control." *The Guardian*, 15 June 2023. www.theguardian.com/society/2023/jun/15/tony-blairs-bet-on-gambling-britain-has-spiralled-out-of-control
14 Colon-Rivera, Hector. "What Is Gambling Disorder?" Psychiatry.org, August 2021. www.psychiatry.org/patients-families/gambling-disorder/what-is-gambling-disorder
15 Moreira, Diana, Andreia Azeredo and Paulo Dias. "Risk Factors for Gambling Disorder: A Systematic Review." *Journal of Gambling Studies* 39, no. 2 (2023): 483–511. doi.org/10.1007/s10899-023-10195-1
16 Ferris, Jackie, and Harold Wynne. "The Canadian Problem Gambling Index." Canadian Centre on Substance Abuse, 19 February 2001
17 "Problem Gambling Screens." Gambling Commission, n.d. www.gamblingcommission.gov.uk/statistics-and-research/publication/problem-gambling-screens
18 "Help for Problems with Gambling." NHS Choices, 8 January 2021. www.nhs.uk/live-well/addiction-support/gambling-addiction/
19 Murali, Vijaya, Rajashree Ray and Mohammed Shaffiullha. "Shopping Addiction." *Advances in Psychiatric Treatment* 18, no. 4 (2012): 263–69. doi.org/10.1192/apt.bp.109.007880
20 Granero, Roser, Fernando Fernández-Aranda, Gemma Mestre-Bach, Trevor Steward, Marta Baño, Amparo del Pino-Gutiérrez, Laura Moragas, et al. "Compulsive Buying Behavior: Clinical Comparison with Other Behavioral Addictions." *Frontiers in Psychology* 7 (2016). doi.org/10.3389/fpsyg.2016.00914
21 Maraz, Aniko, Mark D Griffiths and Zsolt Demetrovics. "The Prevalence of Compulsive Buying: A Meta-analysis." *Addiction* 111, no. 3 (2016): 408–19. doi.org/10.1111/add.13223
22 *British Social Attitudes Survey*. Government Equalities Office, 23 May 2013. www.gov.uk/government/publications/body-confidence-a-rapid-evidence-assessment-of-the-literature
23 *Body Image Report*. Mental Health Foundation, n.d. www.mentalhealth.org.uk/our-work/research/body-image-how-we-think-and-feel-about-our-bodies/body-image-report-introduction
24 Bjornsson, Andri S, Elizabeth R Didie and Katharine A Phillips. "Body Dysmorphic Disorder." *Dialogues in Clinical Neuroscience* 12, no. 2 (2010): 221–32. doi.org/10.31887/dcns.2010.12.2/abjornsson

25 "Table 23, DSM-IV to DSM-5 Body Dysmorphic Disorder Comparison – DSM-5 ..." DSM-5 Changes: Implications for Child Serious Emotional Disturbance, June 2016. www.ncbi.nlm.nih.gov/books/NBK519712/table/ch3.t19/

26 *The Knowledge Project*, episode no. 159, Dr Anna Lembke: "Between Pleasure and Pain", n.d.

27 Granero, Roser, Fernando Fernández-Aranda, Gemma Mestre-Bach, Trevor Steward, Marta Baño, Amparo del Pino-Gutiérrez, Laura Moragas, et al. "Compulsive Buying Behavior: Clinical Comparison with Other Behavioral Addictions." *Frontiers in Psychology* 7 (2016). doi.org/10.3389/fpsyg.2016.00914

28 Fehrman, Elaine, Vincent Egan, Alexander N Gorban, Jeremy Levesley, Evgeny M Mirkes, and Awaz K Muhammad. *Personality Traits and Drug Consumption*, 2019. doi.org/10.1007/978-3-030-10442-9

29 Khantzian, Edward J. "The Self-Medication Hypothesis of Substance Use Disorders: A Reconsideration and Recent Applications." *Harvard Review of Psychiatry* 4, no. 5 (1997): 231–44. doi.org/10.3109/10673229709030550

Searching for the Highs

1 *The Neurobiology of Drug Addiction*, 2007. nida.nih.gov/sites/default/files/1922-the-neurobiology-of-drug-addiction.pdf.

2 Olds, James, and Peter Milner. "Positive Reinforcement Produced by Electrical Stimulation of Septal Area and Other Regions of Rat Brain." *Journal of Comparative and Physiological Psychology* 47, no. 6 (1954): 419–27. doi.org/10.1037/h0058775

3 Olds, James. "Pleasure Centers in the Brain." *Scientific American* 195, no. 4 (1956): 105–17. doi.org/10.1038/scientificamerican1056-105

4 Fisher, Helen, Arthur Aron, and Lucy L Brown. "Romantic Love: An fMRI Study of a Neural Mechanism for Mate Choice." *Journal of Comparative Neurology* 493, no. 1 (2005): 58–62. doi.org/10.1002/cne.20772

5 Earp, Brian D, Olga A Wudarczyk, Bennett Foddy and Julian Savulescu. "Addicted to Love: What Is Love Addiction and When Should It Be Treated?" *Philosophy, Psychiatry & Psychology* 24, no. 1 (2017): 77–92. doi.org/10.1353/ppp.2017.0011

6 Blum, Kenneth, Tonia Werner, Stefanie Carnes, Patrick Carnes, Abdalla Bowirrat, John Giordano, Marlene Oscar-Berman and Mark Gold. "Sex, Drugs, and Rock 'n' Roll: Hypothesizing Common Mesolimbic Activation as a Function of Reward Gene Polymorphisms." *Journal of Psychoactive Drugs* 44, no. 1 (2012): 38–55. doi.org/10.1080/02791072.2012.662112

7 Taylor, Petroc. "Mobile Network Subscriptions Worldwide 2028." Statista, 19 July 2023. www.statista.com/statistics/330695/number-of-smartphone-users-worldwide/

8 Krach, Sören. "The Rewarding Nature of Social Interactions." *Frontiers in Behavioral Neuroscience*, 2010. doi.org/10.3389/fnbeh.2010.00022

9 Hristova, Dayana, Suzana Jovicic, Barbara Göbl, Sara de Freitas and Thomas Slunecko. "'Why Did We Lose Our Snapchat Streak?'. Social Media Gamification and Metacommunication." *Computers in Human Behavior Reports* 5 (2022): 100172. doi.org/10.1016/j.chbr.2022.100172

10 Satici, Seydi Ahmet, Emine Gocet Tekin, M Engin Deniz and Begum Satici. "Doomscrolling Scale: Its Association with Personality Traits, Psychological Distress, Social Media Use, and Wellbeing." *Applied Research in Quality of Life* 18, no. 2 (2022): 833–47. doi.org/10.1007/s11482-022-10110-7

11 Koepp, M J, R N Gunn, A D Lawrence, V J Cunningham, A Dagher, T Jones, D J Brooks, C J Bench and P M Grasby. "Evidence for Striatal Dopamine Release during a Video Game." *Nature* 393, no. 6682 (1998): 266–68. doi.org/10.1038/30498

12 Polish, Joe, and Gabor Maté. "BEST Explanation of Addiction I've Ever Heard: Dr Gabor Maté." YouTube, 2021. https://www.youtube.com/watch?v=AAJhI2egVtw

13 Joutsa, Juho, Jarkko Johansson, Solja Niemelä, Antti Ollikainen, Mika M Hirvonen, Petteri Piepponen, Eveliina Arponen, et al. "Mesolimbic Dopamine Release Is Linked to Symptom Severity in Pathological Gambling." *NeuroImage* 60, no. 4 (2012): 1992–99. doi.org/10.1016/j.neuroimage.2012.02.006

14 Linnet, J, E Peterson, D J Doudet, A Gjedde and A Møller. "Dopamine Release in Ventral Striatum of Pathological Gamblers Losing Money." *Acta Psychiatrica Scandinavica* 122, no. 4 (2010): 326–33. doi.org/10.1111/j.1600-0447.2010.01591.x

15 Skinner, Burrhus Frederic. *Science and Human Behavior*. New York: Free Press, 1953

16 Linnet, Jakob, Kim Mouridsen, Ericka Peterson, Arne Møller, Doris Jeanne Doudet and Albert Gjedde. "Striatal Dopamine Release Codes Uncertainty in Pathological Gambling." *Psychiatry Research: Neuroimaging* 204, no. 1 (2012): 55–60. doi.org/10.1016/j.pscychresns.2012.04.012

17 Anselme, Patrick, and Mike J Robinson. "What Motivates Gambling Behavior? Insight into Dopamine's Role." *Frontiers in Behavioral Neuroscience* 7 (2013). doi.org/10.3389/fnbeh.2013.00182

18 Rick, Scott I, Beatriz Pereira and Katherine A Burson. "The Benefits of Retail Therapy: Making Purchase Decisions Reduces Residual Sadness." *Journal of Consumer Psychology* 24, no. 3 (2013): 373–80. doi.org/10.1016/j.jcps.2013.12.004

19 Granero, Roser, Fernando Fernández-Aranda, Gemma Mestre-Bach, Trevor Steward, Marta Baño, Amparo del Pino-Gutiérrez, Laura Moragas, et al. "Compulsive Buying Behavior: Clinical Comparison with Other Behavioral Addictions." *Frontiers in Psychology* 7 (2016). doi.org/10.3389/fpsyg.2016.00914

20 Haupt, Angela. "Psychology Behind Online Shopping: Why It's So Addicting." *TIME*, 26 July 2022. time.com/6200717/online-shopping-psychology-explained/

Is it Ever Enough?

1 King, Daniel L, Madeleine C Herd and Paul H Delfabbro. "Tolerance in Internet Gaming Disorder: A Need for Increasing Gaming Time or Something Else?" *Journal of Behavioral Addictions* 6, no. 4 (2017): 525–33. doi.org/10.1556/2006.6.2017.072

2 "Facing Addiction in America: The Surgeon General's Report on Alcohol, Drugs and Health." Washington, D.C.: U.S. Department of Health & Human Services, Office of the Surgeon General, 2016. www.ncbi.nlm.nih.gov/books/NBK424849/#ch2.s8

3 "Facing Addiction in America: The Surgeon General's Report on Alcohol, Drugs and Health." Washington, D.C.: U.S. Department of Health & Human Services, Office of the Surgeon General, 2016

4 "Drugs and the Brain." National Institutes of Health, 22 March 2022. www.nida.nih.gov/publications/drugs-brains-behavior-science-addiction/drugs-brain

5 "The Science of Addiction." National Institute on Drug Abuse, 2020. www.nida.nih.gov/sites/default/files/soa.pdf

6 "Facing Addiction in America: The Surgeon General's Report on Alcohol, Drugs and Health." Washington, D.C.: U.S. Department of Health & Human Services, Office of the Surgeon General, 2016

7 MacKey, Boris. "The Addiction Cycle." Rehab 4 Addiction, 26 July 2021. www.rehab4addiction.co.uk/resources/addiction-cycle

8 "The Addiction Cycle: What Are the Stages of Addiction?" American Addiction Centers, 21 October 2022. www.americanaddictioncenters.org/the-addiction-cycle

9 Juser. "4 Behaviors That Occur during the Cycle of Addiction: Blog." Solstice Pacific. Accessed 11 November 2023. www.pacificsolstice.com/blog/4-behaviors-that-occur-during-the-cycle-of-addiction

10 Nash, J. "A Guide to Breaking the Cycle of Addiction." ALYST Health, 14 December 2022. www.alysthealth.com/guide-to-breaking-cycle-of-addiction/

11 "What Is Process Addiction & Types of Addictive Behaviors?" American Addiction Centers, 11 August 2023. www.americanaddictioncenters.org/behavioral-addictions

12 Sussman, Steven Yale. *The Cambridge Handbook of Substance and Behavioral Addictions*. Cambridge: Cambridge University Press, 2020

13 Grant, Jon E, Judson A Brewer and Marc N Potenza. "The Neurobiology of Substance and Behavioral Addictions." *CNS Spectrums* 11, no. 12 (2006): 924–30. doi.org/10.1017/s109285290001511x

14 Brickman, P, and D T Campbell. "Hedonic relativism and planning the good society." In M H Appley (ed.), *Adaptation level theory: A symposium* (New York: Academic Press, 1971), 287–302

15 Frederick, S, and G Loewenstein. "Hedonic adaptation." In D Kahneman, E Diener and N Schwarz (eds.), *Well-Being: The Foundations of Hedonic Psychology* (Russell Sage Foundation, 1999), 302–329

16 Svanberg, Jenny. "You Can Teach an Old Dog New Tricks." Essay. In *The Psychology of Addiction* (London; New York: Routledge, Taylor et Francis Group, 2018), 63

The Lows of Addiction: What Comes Up, Must Come Down

1 Maslow, Abraham H. *Religions, Values, and Peak-Experiences*. United States: Stellar Books, 2014

2 Maslow, Abraham H, and Robert Frager. *Motivation and Personality*. New Delhi: Pearson Education, 1987

3 Tedeschi, Richard G, and Lawrence G Calhoun. *Posttraumatic Growth: Positive Changes in the Aftermath of Crisis*. Edited by Crystal L Park. New York: Taylor and Francis Group, 1998

4 Taylor, Steve. "The Peak at the Nadir: Psychological Turmoil as the Trigger for Awakening Experiences." *International Journal of Transpersonal Studies* 32, no. 2 (2013): 1–12. doi.org/10.24972/ijts.2013.32.2.1

5 Joseph, Stephen. *What Doesn't Kill Us: The New Psychology of Post-Traumatic Growth*. New York: Basic Books, 2012

6 Joseph, Stephen, Ruth Williams and William Yule. "Changes in Outlook Following Disaster: The Preliminary Development of a Measure to Assess Positive and Negative Responses." *Journal of Traumatic Stress* 6, no. 2 (1993): 271–79. doi.org/10.1002/jts.2490060209

7 Stagg, R. "The Nadir Experience: Crisis, Transition, and Growth." *Journal of Transpersonal Psychology* 46, no. 1 (2014): 72–91

8 Taylor, Steve. *Out of the Darkness: From Turmoil to Transformation*. London: Hay House, 2011

9 Taylor, Steve. "Transformation through Suffering." *Journal of Humanistic Psychology* 52, no. 1 (2012): 30–52. doi.org/10.1177/0022167811404944

10 Tedeschi, Richard G, and Lawrence G Calhoun. *Posttraumatic Growth: Positive Changes in the Aftermath of Crisis*. Edited by Crystal L Park. New York: Taylor and Francis Group, 1998

11 Stagg, R. "The Nadir Experience: Crisis, Transition, and Growth." *Journal of Transpersonal Psychology* 46, no. 1 (2014): 72–91

12 Foster, Steven, and Meredith Little. *The Roaring of the Sacred River: The Wilderness Quest for Vision and Self-Healing*. New York: Prentice Hall Press, 1989

13 Fosh, Talitha, and Francis Lickerish. Personal interview for *Hooked*, 12 April 2023

Can We Handle the Truth?

1 Bennett, Matthew D, and Rick McNeese. "Introduction to Substance Abuse." First Step Recovery, Inc., 10 September 2023

2 Bailey, Ryan, and Jose Pico. "Defense Mechanisms." StatPearls, 22 May 2023. www.ncbi.nlm.nih.gov/books/NBK559106/

3 "Projection." *Psychology Today*. Accessed 12 September 2023. www.psychologytoday.com/gb/basics/projection

4 Bennett, Matthew D, and Rick McNeese. "Introduction to Substance Abuse." First Step Recovery, Inc., 10 September 2023

5 "APA Dictionary of Psychology." American Psychological Association. Accessed 11 November 2023. dictionary.apa.org/Denial

6 Rinn, William, Nitigna Desai, Harold Rosenblatt and David R Gastfriend. "Addiction Denial and Cognitive Dysfunction." *Journal of Neuropsychiatry and Clinical Neurosciences* 14, no. 1 (2002): 52–57. doi.org/10.1176/jnp.14.1.52

7 Mcleod, Saul. "Defense Mechanisms in Psychology Explained (+ Examples)." Simply Psychology, 24 October 2023. www.simplypsychology.org/defense-mechanisms.html

8 Tyrrell, Patrick, Seneca Harberger, Caroline Schoo and Waquar Siddiqui. "Kubler-Ross Stages of Dying and Subsequent Models of Grief." StatPearls, 26 February 2023. www.ncbi.nlm.nih.gov/books/NBK507885/

9 Bailey, Ryan, and Jose Pico. "Defense Mechanisms." StatPearls, 22 May 2023. www.ncbi.nlm.nih.gov/books/NBK559106/

10 Svanberg, Jenny. "But Addicts Are All in Denial! How Can You Help Someone If They Don't Want Help." Essay. In *The Psychology of Addiction* (London; New York: Routledge, Taylor et Francis Group, 2018), 64–66

11 Anderson, Charity. "Addiction Denial: Symptoms, Behaviors & How to Help." Edited by Amelia Sharp and Ryan Kelley. American Addiction Centers, 22 August 2023. www.americanaddictioncenters.org/rehab-guide/addiction-denial

12 Rinn, William, Nitigna Desai, Harold Rosenblatt and David R Gastfriend. "Addiction Denial and Cognitive Dysfunction." *Journal of Neuropsychiatry and Clinical Neurosciences* 14, no. 1 (2002): 52–57. doi.org/10.1176/jnp.14.1.52

13 Fosh, Talitha, and Francis Lickerish. Personal interview for *Hooked*, 12 April 2023

14 U.S. Department of Health and Human Services and Elinore F McCance-Katz, *Enhancing Motivation for Change in Substance Use Disorder Treatment* (2019)

15 Department of Health and Human Services and Arnold M Washton, *Approaches to Drug Abuse Counselling* (2019)

16 Maté, Gabor. "A Word to Families, Friends and Caregivers." Essay. In *In the Realm of Hungry Ghosts: Close Encounters with Addiction* (London: Vermillion, an imprint of Ebury Publishing, 2018), 378

17 "FAQ – Al-Anon Family Groups." Al-Anon, 17 April 2023. www.al-anonuk.org.uk/getting-help/faq/

18 Maté, Gabor. "A Word to Families, Friends and Caregivers." Essay. In *In the Realm of Hungry Ghosts: Close Encounters with Addiction* (London: Vermillion, an imprint of Ebury Publishing, 2018), 380

19 Heshmat, Shahram. "The Role of Denial in Addiction." *Psychology Today*, 13 November 2018. www.psychologytoday.com/gb/blog/science-choice/201811/the-role-denial-in-addiction

Breaking the Patterns

1 Fennell, Melanie J. "Low Self-Esteem: A Cognitive Perspective." *Behavioural and Cognitive Psychotherapy* 25, no. 1 (1997): 1–26. doi.org/10.1017/s1352465800015368

2 "Cognitive Behavioral Model of Low Self-Esteem (Fennell, 1997)." Psychology Tools. Accessed 18 September 2023. www.psychologytools.com/resource/cognitive-behavioral-model-of-low-self-esteem-fennell-1997/

3 "Core Beliefs, Attitudes & Rules in CBT." Psychology Therapy, 2 July 2023. www.psychologytherapy.co.uk/blog/core-beliefs-and-attitudes-rules-and-assumptions-in-cognitive-behavioural-therapy-cbt/

4 Fenn, Kristina, and Majella Byrne. "The Key Principles of Cognitive Behavioural Therapy." *InnovAiT: Education and inspiration for general practice* 6, no. 9 (2013): 579–85. doi.org/10.1177/1755738012471029

5 Cowan, Henry R, Dan P McAdams and Vijay A Mittal. "Core Beliefs in Healthy Youth and Youth at Ultra High-Risk for Psychosis: Dimensionality

and Links to Depression, Anxiety, and Attenuated Psychotic Symptoms." *Development and Psychopathology* 31, no. 1 (2018): 379–92. doi.org/10.1017/s0954579417001912

6 Beck, Judith S. *Cognitive behavior therapy: Basics and beyond.* 3rd ed. New York: The Guilford Press, 2021

7 Martiros, Nuné, Alexandra A Burgess, and Ann M Graybiel. "Inversely Active Striatal Projection Neurons and Interneurons Selectively Delimit Useful Behavioral Sequences." *Current Biology* 28, no. 4 (2018). doi.org/10.1016/j.cub.2018.01.031

8 Jeffrey Gaines, Ph.D. "How Are Habits Formed? The Psychology of Habit Formation." Positive Psychology, 20 September 2023. www.positivepsychology.com/how-habits-are-formed/

9 Leotti, Lauren A, Sheena S Iyengar and Kevin N Ochsner. "Born to Choose: The Origins and Value of the Need for Control." *Trends in Cognitive Sciences* 14, no. 10 (2010): 457–63. doi.org/10.1016/j.tics.2010.08.001

10 Antonatos, Lydia. "Fear of Change: Causes, Getting Help, & Ways to Cope." Edited by Rajy Albuhosn. Choosing Therapy, 29 April 2022. www.choosingtherapy.com/fear-of-change/

11 Lewis, Ralph. "What Actually Is a Belief? And Why Is It So Hard To Change?" Edited by Ekua Hagan. *Psychology Today*, 7 October 2018. www.psychologytoday.com/gb/blog/finding-purpose/201810/what-actually-is-belief-and-why-is-it-so-hard-change

12 Lembke, Anna. "Dopamine Fasting." Essay. In *Dopamine Nation: Finding Balance in the Age of Indulgence* (London: Headline Publishing Group, 2023), 76–77

13 Lawler, Moira. "How to Do a Digital Detox." Edited by Seth Gillihan. Everyday Health, 4 August 2023. www.everydayhealth.com/emotional-health/how-to-do-a-digital-detox-without-unplugging-completely/

14 Cherry, Kendra. "The Benefits of Doing a Digital Detox." Edited by Claudia Chaves. Verywell Mind, 31 October 2023. www.verywellmind.com/why-and-how-to-do-a-digital-detox-4771321

15 "Stages of Change Model." Loma Linda School of Medicine. Accessed 3 October 2023. www.medicine.llu.edu/academics/resources/stages-change-model

16 Prochaska, James O, and Wayne F Velicer. "The Transtheoretical Model of Health Behavior Change." *American Journal of Health Promotion* 12, no. 1 (1997): 38–48. doi.org/10.4278/0890-1171-12.1.38

17 Jeffrey Gaines, Ph.D. "How Are Habits Formed? The Psychology of Habit Formation." Positive Psychology, 20 September 2023. www.positivepsychology.com/how-habits-are-formed/

18 Brewer, Judson. "How to Break Up with Your Bad Habits." *Harvard Business Review*, 16 December 2019. hbr.org/2019/12/how-to-break-up-with-your-bad-habits

19 Gardner, Benjamin, Phillippa Lally and Jane Wardle. "Making Health Habitual: The Psychology of 'Habit-Formation' and General Practice." *British Journal of General Practice* 62, no. 605 (2012): 664–66. doi.org/10.3399/bjgp12x659466

20 Lally, Phillippa, Jane Wardle and Benjamin Gardner. "Experiences of Habit Formation: A Qualitative Study." *Psychology, Health & Medicine* 16, no. 4 (2011): 484–89. doi.org/10.1080/13548506.2011.555774

21 Gardner, Benjamin, Phillippa Lally and Jane Wardle. "Making Health Habitual: The Psychology of 'Habit-Formation' and General Practice." *British Journal of General Practice* 62, no. 605 (2012): 664–66. doi.org/10.3399/bjgp12x659466

22 Frothingham, Scott. "How Long Does It Actually Take to Form a New Habit?" Edited by Timothy J Legg. Healthline, 24 October 2019. www.psychcentral.com/health/need-to-form-a-new-habit

23 Lally, Phillippa, Cornelia H van Jaarsveld, Henry W Potts and Jane Wardle. "How Are Habits Formed: Modelling Habit Formation in the Real World." *European Journal of Social Psychology* 40, no. 6 (2009): 998–1009. doi.org/10.1002/ejsp.674

24 Wood, Alex M, Jeffrey J Froh and Adam W A Geraghty. "Gratitude and Well-Being: A Review and Theoretical Integration." *Clinical Psychology Review* 30, no. 7 (2010): 890–905. doi.org/10.1016/j.cpr.2010.03.005

25 Fosh, Talitha, and Cosmo Duff Gordon. Personal interview for *Hooked*, 5 April 2023

26 Hari, Johann. "Everything You Think You Know About Addiction Is Wrong." TED Talk, June 2015

27 Alexander, Bruce K, Barry L Beyerstein, Patricia F Hadaway and Robert B Coambs. "Effect of Early and Later Colony Housing on Oral Ingestion

of Morphine in Rats." *Pharmacology Biochemistry and Behavior* 15, no. 4 (1981): 571–76. doi.org/10.1016/0091-3057(81)90211-2

Dealing With the Feelings

1 Tseng, Julie, and Jordan Poppenk. "Brain Meta-State Transitions Demarcate Thoughts across Task Contexts Exposing the Mental Noise of Trait Neuroticism." *Nature Communications* 11, no. 1 (2020). doi.org/10.1038/s41467-020-17255-9

2 Maté, Gabor. *In the Realm of Hungry Ghosts: Close Encounters with Addiction*. London: Vermillion, an imprint of Ebury Publishing, 2018

3 Maté, Gabor. "The Keys of Paradise." Essay. In *In the Realm of Hungry Ghosts: Close Encounters with Addiction* (London: Vermillion, an imprint of Ebury Publishing, 2018), 39

4 Fosh, Talitha, and Cosmo Duff Gordon. Personal interview for *Hooked*, 5 April 2023

5 Czeisler, Mark, Rashon I Lane, Emiko Petrosky, Joshua F Wiley, Aleta Christensen, Rashid Njai, Matthew D Weaver, et al. "Mental Health, Substance Use, and Suicidal Ideation during the COVID-19 Pandemic – United States, June 24–30, 2020." *Morbidity and Mortality Weekly Report* 69, no. 32 (2020): 1049–57. doi.org/10.15585/mmwr.mm6932a1

6 Allen, Joshua George, John Romate and Eslavath Rajkumar. "Mindfulness-Based Positive Psychology Interventions: A Systematic Review." *BMC Psychology* 9, no. 1 (2021). doi.org/10.1186/s40359-021-00618-2

7 "Breath Meditation: A Great Way to Relieve Stress." Harvard Health, 15 April 2014. www.health.harvard.edu/mind-and-mood/breath-meditation-a-great-way-to-relieve-stress

8 Kabat-Zinn, Jon. *Full Catastrophe Living: Using the Wisdom of Your Body and Mind to Face Stress, Pain, and Ollness*. New York: Bantam Books, 2013

9 Cox, Janelle. "Finding Peace: 7 Principles of Mindfulness." Edited by Cheryl Crumpler. Psych Central, 30 June 2022. www.psychcentral.com/blog/non-judging-non-striving-and-the-pillars-of-mindfulness-practice#7-principles

10 "9 Attitudes Jon Kabat Zinn." YouTube, mindfulnessgruppen, 2015. www.youtube.com/watch?v=2n7FOBFMvXg

11 "Emotional Wellness Toolkit." National Institutes of Health, 8 August 2022. www.nih.gov/health-information/emotional-wellness-toolkit

12 De-Sola Gutiérrez, José, Fernando Rodríguez de Fonseca and Gabriel Rubio. "Cell-Phone Addiction: A Review." *Frontiers in Psychiatry* 7 (2016). doi.org/10.3389/fpsyt.2016.00175

13 Kerai, Alex. "2023 Cell Phone Usage Statistics: Mornings Are for Notifications." Reviews.org, 30 August 2023. www.reviews.org/mobile/cell-phone-addiction/

14 Liu, Huan, Zhiqing Zhou, Long Huang, Ergang Zhu, Liang Yu and Ming Zhang. "Prevalence of Smartphone Addiction and Its Effects on Subhealth and Insomnia: A Cross-Sectional Study among Medical Students." *BMC Psychiatry* 22, no. 1 (2022). doi.org/10.1186/s12888-022-03956-6

15 Maté, Gabor. "The Four Steps, Plus One." Essay. In *In the Realm of Hungry Ghosts: Close Encounters with Addiction* (London: Vermillion, an imprint of Ebury Publishing, 2018), 358–59

16 Ledochowski, Larissa, Gerhard Ruedl, Adrian H Taylor and Martin Kopp. "Acute Effects of Brisk Walking on Sugary Snack Cravings in Overweight People, Affect and Responses to a Manipulated Stress Situation and to a Sugary Snack Cue: A Crossover Study." *PLOS ONE* 10, no. 3 (2015). doi.org/10.1371/journal.pone.0119278

Seeking Help and Recovery

1 "Historical Data." Alcoholics Anonymous, Great Britain. Accessed 12 November 2023. www.alcoholics-anonymous.org.uk/about-aa/historical-data

2 "Our Approach." SMART Recovery, 2022. www.smartrecovery.org/our-approach/

3 "ABC Crash Course." SMART Recovery, 2022. www.smartrecovery.org/smart-recovery-toolbox/abc-crash-course/

4 Fosh, Talitha, and Rebecca McGurrell. Personal interview for *Hooked*, 30 May 2023

5 Margarita Tartakovsky, MS. "Art Therapy Exercises to Try at Home." Psych Central, 6 August 2011. www.psychcentral.com/blog/art-therapy-exercises-to-try-at-home#1

6 Malchiodi, Cathy A. *Handbook of Art Therapy*, second edition. New York: Guilford Publications, 2012

7 Stuckey, Heather L, and Jeremy Nobel. "The Connection Between Art, Healing, and Public Health: A Review of Current Literature." *American Journal of Public Health* 100, no. 2 (2010): 254–63. doi.org/10.2105/ajph.2008.156497

8 Malchiodi, Cathy. *The Art Therapy Sourcebook*. Chicago, IL: Contemporary, 1999

9 Aletraris, Lydia, Maria Paino, Mary Bond Edmond, Paul M Roman and Brian E Bride. "The Use of Art and Music Therapy in Substance Abuse Treatment Programs." *Journal of Addictions Nursing* 25, no. 4 (2014): 190–96. doi.org/10.1097/jan.0000000000000048

10 "How We Work." Music Therapy Works. Accessed 12 November 2023. www.musictherapyworks.co.uk/what-happens-in-a-music-therapy-session

11 "Music Therapy: Using the Power of Music." British Association for Music Therapy. Accessed 12 November 2023. www.bamt.org/content/5078/Live/document/What%20is%20Music%20Therapy%20leaflet.pdf

12 Hohmann, Louisa, Joke Bradt, Thomas Stegemann, and Stefan Koelsch. "Effects of Music Therapy and Music-Based Interventions in the Treatment of Substance Use Disorders: A Systematic Review." *PLOS ONE* 12, no. 11 (2017). doi.org/10.1371/journal.pone.0187363

13 Witte, Martina de, Ana da Pinho, Geert-Jan Stams, Xavier Moonen, Arjan E R Bos and Susan van Hooren. "Music Therapy for Stress Reduction: A Systematic Review and Meta-Analysis." *Health Psychology Review* 16, no. 1 (2020): 134–59. doi.org/10.1080/17437199.2020.1846580

14 Ghetti, Claire, Xi-Jing Chen, Annette K Brenner, Laurien G Hakvoort, Lars Lien, Jorg Fachner and Christian Gold. "Music Therapy for People with Substance Use Disorders." *Cochrane Database of Systematic Reviews* 2022, no. 5 (2022). doi.org/10.1002/14651858.cd012576.pub3

15 Baikie, Karen A, and Kay Wilhelm. "Emotional and Physical Health Benefits of Expressive Writing." *Advances in Psychiatric Treatment* 11, no. 5 (2005): 338–46. doi.org/10.1192/apt.11.5.338

One Foot in Front of the Other

1 Melemis, Steven M. "Relapse Prevention and the Five Rules of Recovery." *The Yale Journal of Biology and Medicine* 88, no. 3 (September 2015): 325–32

2 "Treatment and Recovery." National Institutes of Health, 25 September 2023. www.nida.nih.gov/publications/drugs-brains-behavior-science-addiction/treatment-recovery

3 Smyth, B P, J Barry, E Keenan and K Ducray. "Lapse and Relapse Following Inpatient Treatment of Opiate Dependence." *Irish Medical Journal* 103, no. 6 (June 2010): 176–79

4 Liese, Bruce S, and Aaron T Beck. *Cognitive-Behavioral Therapy of Addictive Disorders*. New York: London, 2022

5 Stewart, Jane. "Pathways to Relapse: The Neurobiology of Drug- and Stress-Induced Relapse to Drug-Taking." *Journal of Psychiatry and Neuroscience* 25, no. 2 (2000): 125–36

6 Stewart, Jane. "Psychological and Neural Mechanisms of Relapse." *Philosophical Transactions of the Royal Society B: Biological Sciences* 363, no. 1507 (2008): 3147–58. doi.org/10.1098/rstb.2008.0084

7 Sinha, Rajita. "How Does Stress Increase Risk of Drug Abuse and Relapse?" *Alcohol Research* 34, no. 4 (2012): 432–40

8 Jupp, B, E Krstew, G Dezsi and A J Lawrence. "Discrete Cue-Conditioned Alcohol-Seeking after Protracted Abstinence: Pattern of Neural Activation and Involvement of Orexin$_1$ Receptors." *British Journal of Pharmacology* 162, no. 4 (2011): 880–89. doi.org/10.1111/j.1476-5381.2010.01088.x

9 Perry, Christina J, Isabel Zbukvic, Jee Hyun Kim and Andrew J Lawrence. "Role of Cues and Contexts on Drug-Seeking Behaviour." *British Journal of Pharmacology* 171, no. 20 (2014): 4636–72. doi.org/10.1111/bph.12735

10 Marlatt, Alan, and Judith R Gordon. *Relapse Prevention: Maintenance Strategies in the Treatment of Addictive Behaviors*. New York: Guilford Press, 1985

11 Marlatt, G Alan. "Taxonomy of High-Risk Situations for Alcohol Relapse: Evolution and Development of a Cognitive-Behavioral Model." *Addiction* 91, no. 12 (1996): 37–50. doi.org/10.1046/j.1360-0443.91.12s1.15.x

12 Melemis, Steven M. "Relapse Prevention and the Five Rules of Recovery." *The Yale Journal of Biology and Medicine* 88, no. 3 (September 2015): 325–32

13 Fosh, Talitha, and Francis Lickerish. Personal interview for *Hooked*, 12 April 2023

14 Lembke, Anna. "Radical Honesty." Essay. In *Dopamine Nation: Finding Balance in the Age of Indulgence* (London: Headline Publishing Group, 2023), 182

15 "Relapse, Verb – Definition, Pictures, Pronunciation and Usage Notes." *Oxford Learner's Dictionary*, 2023. www.oxfordlearnersdictionaries.com/definition/american_english/relapse_2

ABOUT THE AUTHOR

Talitha Fosh is a qualified psychotherapist, and a member of both the British Association of Counselling and Psychotherapy (BACP) and Federation of Drug and Alcohol Practitioners (FDAP) since 2019. Drawing on her personal journey of recovery from addiction, she brings a unique perspective to her private practice, where she assists clients dealing with addiction and eating disorders. Talitha is also adept at addressing challenges related to anxiety, relationships and attachment styles. As a qualified yoga teacher, she recognizes the synergy of movement and therapy in achieving balance, healing and happiness.

Beyond her clinical practice, Talitha has conducted workshops on attachment styles and co-hosted a podcast with Holly Ramsay. She took part in a national tour with Gurls Talk, conducting mental health workshops in various schools across the country. *Hooked* is her debut book, a project fuelled by her deep passion for the subject. Through sharing her experiences, Talitha aspires to make a meaningful contribution to the wellbeing of others.

Talitha's private practice, "Therapised", is based in West London, where she also lives with her husband.

ACKNOWLEDGEMENTS

First I want to thank Cosmo and Francis, not only for your contributions to this book but also for saving me when I was in my darkest times. Thank you to Karla, my therapist, for continuously helping me to change and grow.

I want to thank Rebecca for her constant support and motivation – I am very lucky to call you my colleague. To Adwoa, who helped me realize that being sober could be fun – you are my inspiration.

To Shona, who, without you, my career would not be what it is today. Your encouragement and wisdom has helped shaped the person I am today, and this book wouldn't be what it is without your support.

Thank you to everyone on the Watkins publishing team – to Lucy and Oscar for taking the risk and believing in me and this book.

To my mum and dad, family and friends. Thank you for bearing with me for so many years. For allowing me to take my time to figure out who I am with your unconditional love and support. To my brother Max, thank you for being my best friend and support, even through my lowest moments.

And finally, my husband, Dr Nathan Cohen-Fosh. Without you, this book would literally not have been possible and I am beyond grateful for your patience and encouragement. Thank you for sacrificing so much of your time to help me write, for your continued guidance, endless love and generous spirit. Finally, thank you for believing in me when I found it hardest to.